THE DEFIANT

STAR LEGEND BOOK SIX

J.J. GREEN

INFINITEBOOK

1

Spiral City, Java, glowed in the morning sun. Once, it had been a sea of shacks. Entire families had lived in single-room houses made from corrugated iron, sharing a single, stinking pit toilet with hundreds of others. Water had come from a standpipe and it often made you sick. Danger stalked the slum dwellers: stray dogs that transmitted a terrible, fatal disease through their bites; fires that spread faster than anyone could run; bad men in shadows, waiting to snatch an unwary child.

Setia Zees gazed out across the cityscape from a steep street in the poor, hilly quarter, ruminating on how everything looked different now. After the Britannic Alliance starship had sent back revelatory scientific information from deep space, things had begun to change. Setia didn't understand much about it, but apparently the knowledge had allowed scientists and engineers to develop new technologies—technologies for transportation, farming, medicine, building...so many things.

And the spirals had begun to appear in her home town. She recalled the first gravity-defying building going up in the city center. Everyone had marveled as each thick, tall story appeared, sweeping around a wide curve, hanging impossibly in the air, supported only by the central base. When the building was complete at fifteen stories high, a machine had applied a brilliant orange, reflective coating, turning the entire structure into a beacon, a burning flame in the dull, gray scene emblazoned with the name of the multi-national corporation owners. The name stuck in minds near and far, as was exactly the intention.

As she grew from a child to an adolescent, the trend for spiral structures had caught on. Shining edifices in a myriad of colors had sprung up everywhere. The form appealed to her countrymen, Setia guessed. She had little access to news from other countries, but she hadn't seen pictures or reports about similar buildings. And so Spiral City had earned its unofficial name.

She was proud of the place. It was home, all she'd ever known, and it would break her heart to leave it. But she had no choice if she wanted to live.

"Setia!"

The urgent whisper had come from somewhere to her right. She spied a childhood friend in the darkness between two shacks.

"Aulia? What are you doing? Why are you hiding?"

"Don't look at me! Pratam has sent someone after you. He knows you're here."

Aulia was gone.

Her dear, old friend had risked her life to protect her. If word ever got back to Pratam about the warning, Aulia's life would also be forfeit.

Setia was already running. She went downhill, hoping she wasn't heading toward her attacker.

She pushed past the barefoot pedestrians blocking her way. Seniors, children, and the unemployed were out on errands or shopping. The street was thick with them. Roadside vendors created more obstacles, though they would be obstacles for her pursuers too.

Who was coming after her? Aulia hadn't said. Would it be muscle-bound Soleh, Pratam's right-hand man and brute enforcer of his will? Or perhaps it would be Yuda, the silent assassin, murderer of the powerful, the elite whose deaths must be quiet and of undefined causes.

She risked a glance over her shoulder.

It was Soleh.

She hadn't seen the man, only the effects of his progress. At the top of the street, in the dusty haze, the crowd was violently parting. A channel had formed, its edges made of crushed, stumbling passersby. Shouts of protest and alarm leaked through the hubbub.

Setia stepped up her pace. As she vaulted a low table her toe knocked a street magician's cards from his hands. A vulgar curse followed her, something involving the insertion of body parts into ill-considered orifices.

A woman laden with pastries crossed her path. She had no time to dodge. She smashed into her, scattering her wares across the ground. A hungry mob descended and a scuffle ensued.

She felt bad for the woman but the accident should slow Soleh down.

She'd reached the bottom of the hill, where the market petered out to a handful of stalls and the crowd thinned. An alley opened to her left. Side-stepping a beggar sitting cross-legged, his upturned palms level with the dirty rag bound over his eyes, she darted down the alley.

It ran alongside a derelict building, once a vast department store. On the other side stood a building site fence. A green metal constructor suddenly reared beyond it. The machine's rounded head bobbed up and down as its long, articulated arm laid blocks at a breath-taking speed. If she jumped the fence she would be safe from Soleh but in danger from the constructor bots. Humans weren't allowed on building sites. The manufacturers couldn't guarantee the constructors would stop in time before hurting someone.

But maybe she was already safe.

She looked back over her shoulder, panting.

No.

Soleh was kicking the beggar aside. He must have seen her turn off the main street. As their gazes met across the distance, he looked furious. Glistening with sweat, his shirt wide open, his expression black as a thunder cloud, he was probably incensed that she hadn't given herself up and allowed him to kill her without going to all this bother.

She ran.

The alley was long. Both the old department store and the construction site were vast.

When would she reach the end?

She flicked another glance over her shoulder.

Burnap's balls.

Soleh was gaining on her.

She scanned the department store wall.

Bricks.

Bricks.

Some more bricks.

Not a door, a window, or even a vent at ground level. Not a single opening in the blank expanse.

Then the end of the alley grew clear.

Yes!

No.

What she'd thought had been the wall of a street or another alley running across this one was in fact a dead end.

The light dimmed as if illustrating her dismal predicament,

but she had no time to figure out why. Normal brightness quickly returned.

Her only escape was the fence. She would have to take her chance with the constructor whirring and clanking to her right. And she had to do it now, before Soleh reached her.

"Setia Zees?"

A tall, slim figure had appeared from nowhere. She skidded to a halt.

"Burnap's balls, where did you come from?!"

She was sure he hadn't been here a second ago. There was no door he could have stepped from and she assumed he couldn't walk through walls.

Before the man could answer, she said, "Forget it." She leapt for the top of the fence. "Nice to meet you and goodb—"

The strange man tugged sharply on her ankle. She tumbled down, grazing her knees on the rough ground. "What the hell?"

Soleh had reached her. His hands on his muscled hips, his gaze moved from Setia to the interloper. He had to be trying to figure out if the man was friend or foe.

So was Setia.

Judging from the fact he'd prevented her escaping, he was not a friend.

But any port in a storm.

"Thanks for coming to my rescue," she said confidently, edging behind him. "Soleh, as you can see, I'm not alone. I have important and..." she squinted up into the man's enigmatic face "...powerful allies. More important and powerful than Pratam, so you can go back and tell him he'd better forget about me if he knows what's good for him."

"Pratam doesn't give a shit about your friend," Soleh spat. However, he also didn't move a single step forward. "Someone has to pay for the missing merch, and that someone is *you*."

This was what pissed Setia off so much about the whole

affair. None of it was her fault. She'd run drugs for her boss faithfully and reliably for over two years, never missing an appointment, never getting smart-mouthed with the customers—no matter how much they deserved it—never skimming a little off the top and substituting with detergent, as many runners did. Was it her fault she'd been robbed? It had to happen sooner or later. It was one of the inevitable drawbacks of the business. By punishing her he was hurting himself. Reliable runners were hard to come by. But Pratam was as stupid as he was vindictive.

"Fight," said the stranger.

"Whaa...?" She double-checked he was speaking to her, not Soleh. This wasn't how she'd hoped things would go. It would have been better if he told Soleh to go away—infinitely better if he produced a gun and shot him.

The man's dark eyes bored into hers. Dressed in a dark gray suit, his clothes marked him out as one of Spiral City's wealthier citizens, yet there was something not quite right about him. He grabbed her shoulder, his fingers digging into her flesh like steel pins, and dragged her forward until she stood between him and Soleh.

"Fight."

Fight?

Setia's opponent grinned and rubbed the knuckles of one hand into the palm of the other.

"No weapons," said the man in a commanding tone.

Soleh had been obeying orders all his life and he was even dumber than Pratam. He nodded agreement, pulled knives from their sheaths on each side of his torso, bent down and slid them along the ground a couple of meters to his rear.

Setia still had no hope of beating him. Soleh stood head and shoulders taller than her and he was about twice as wide. He was also a killer and practiced brawler, while she'd only been in the usual street fights, mostly bravado and windmilling fists. She'd learned enough to extract herself and run away, which had always seemed to her the wisest response.

The strange man's hand remained on her shoulder. She'd almost forgotten about it in all the excitement, but then an odd feeling emanated from his touch. A sensation flowed from it, a hot, liquid feeling, like blood pouring from a wound, but instead it was flowing *into* her. An energized thrill passed through her, leaving every part of her feeling stronger. Her muscles no longer ached from running, her panting ceased, and her heart rate slowed and steadied. Calmness and confidence suffused her.

Her mouth dropped open and she stared at the man.

Was this some new type of drug? She'd never tried any of Pratam's merchandise. The terrible state of his customers had put her off the stuff for life. But her experience seemed similar to accounts she'd heard.

Still, what good would drugs do against—

As she'd been staring at the stranger, slack-jawed, she glimpsed movement in her peripheral vision. The next thing she knew, her forearm hit something meaty. Soleh had swung for her and she'd blocked him without even thinking about it.

Soleh looked as surprised as she felt.

He threw another fist. Like an automaton, she ducked. As his momentum carried him forward she grabbed his shirt and pulled him closer and down before driving her knee into his nose. He toppled forward and she kicked his knee, buckling it. He screamed and collapsed. She leapt on top of him and locked her leg around his neck, folding her other leg over the first, pulling it tight. Soleh tried to rise but her weight held him down. He tried to prise her from his throat but she squeezed tighter.

In a few seconds, his body went limp.

Setia lay still, numbly wondering what had just happened.

How had she managed to defeat Soleh, Pratam's best

fighter? It had all taken place so quickly. She'd moved as if by instinct.

The man was holding out a hand. She grasped it and he helped her to her feet.

"Come with me, Setia. I have someone I would like you to meet. You are both destined for great things."

2

Patrin Ellis clenched and unclenched his hands as they rested on his knees. He took in a deep breath and then exhaled slowly and evenly, practicing the technique Mam had taught him to ease his racing pulse. It didn't do much good. Sweat prickled his brow and trickled down the back of his neck.

The room was too warm. Why did they have to make it so warm? It was barely autumn outside, let alone winter. There was no need for them to have the heating on.

Carys leaned close and murmured, "You'll do fine. Don't worry."

"I'm not worried," he shot back heatedly. Then, feeling shameful at his outburst, he repeated, more gently, "I'm not really worried. I just wish they would get it over with. Why are they taking so long?"

She shrugged. "These things take a long time. They have to do everything correctly, according to the rules. If they make a mistake it gives his team an opening. You don't want to go through this again, do you?"

"Definitely not."

"Then try to be patient. Answer every question clearly, to the best of your knowledge and memory. You can't do any better than that. It'll be over before you know it."

I wish.

He recognized some of the people in the waiting room, or at least he thought he recognized them. Ten years had passed since he'd seen these boys and girls, and they were not allowed to speak to each other, to exchange names or stories. The evidence had to be as uncorrupted as possible, uninfluenced by other accounts of what had happened.

He and Carys were an exception. They'd lived together since returning to West BI. Any sharing of stories had already taken place, the authorities said, so it didn't matter if they talked to each other. Except they hadn't shared anything. Neither he nor Carys ever mentioned that time. He supposed she didn't want to bring up the subject any more than he did. Why go over something that made your guts clamp down in painful knots whenever you thought about it? There was nothing either of them could say that would change the past.

Kayla was lucky. She'd been so young then, she been ruled out as a reliable witness.

The door slid open in a quiet *whoosh*, loud in the silent room.

"Patrin Ellis," said the official, reading from an interface.

"Good luck," Carys whispered as he stood up.

He didn't look back at her as he left.

The official led him along a narrow passageway and up some steps. At the top of the steps stood an open door, light spilling from it. The low hum of quiet voices also leaked out. He stepped through the opening and the voices quietened to silence. The door snicked closed behind him. The official had disappeared. He was alone inside a booth with transparent plastic walls.

The judge sat highest in the room, on a platform behind a

polished desk. Men and women in suits were behind more desks. He recognized one of them: Mr Barnaby, who had helped him prepare for today. Beyond the lawyers was the audience, perched on rows of benches, squashed together. The place was packed.

His gaze roved the faces.

Where was she?

Then he saw her.

Mam.

She smiled and gave a little wave. His nervousness fell away.

Sitting next to her was her boyfriend, TJ. Mam always called him by his surname, Wright. He wasn't sure why. He liked TJ. He was a good guy. Good for Mam. Steady and kind. She needed someone like that.

Just be honest about what you remember, she'd said. *That's all. Just tell them what happened.*

"Would the witness please be seated," the judge snapped.

Shit.

He slid into the seat, embarrassed. Everyone was staring at him. They must think he's an idiot.

He went through the formalities, swearing to tell the truth. There were no mics he could see. He guessed the see-through walls would pick up his response as he gave his replies.

Mr Barnaby was suddenly in front of the booth. Patrin braced himself for the questions about to come.

Then he saw the accused.

Sitting at the defense barristers' desks was a man whose face made him instantly fearful. The man looked much older, thinner, and paler than Patrin remembered, and his thick, dark hair had been replaced by strands of silvery gray. It was no wonder he hadn't recognized him at first. But now he looked closely, he was in no doubt it was Summoner Seba.

Like so many Crusaders, Seba had vanished into the ether after the Alliance had re-taken the Isles, turning the tide of the war, pushing back the cultists' darkness, and sparking the return to modern civilization and rationality. The last time Patrin had seen him, Seba had been coordinating the break-up of the camp in the Australian desert. In the light from flickering lamps, the children's captors had been moving to and fro, hastily collapsing the tents and gathering supplies, loading them onto horse-drawn wagons, ready to flee into the desert.

So much had happened that night and over the following days. Patrin preferred not to recall the memories, but Barnaby's questions mostly focused on earlier times. He answered as well as he could. He had to talk about specific instances he'd seen Seba giving orders and punishing children through beating or starvation.

After each answer, Barnaby would very briefly pause and glance at the jury.

The court was an old-fashioned way of running Seba's trial. Modern trials didn't take place in courtrooms with everyone physically present anymore. No one had to leave their home or office to give their testimony. But the Crusader war crimes trials were held differently as a concession to their culture and beliefs.

He would have preferred to be at home and not on show to hundreds of people.

"No further questions, Your Honor," said Barnaby.

Patrin relaxed and then tensed. Now it was the other side's turn. These questions would be harder. Barnaby had said Seba's team would try to confuse and trick him to make him look stupid or a liar.

Just tell them what happened.

"Patrin," said the woman who had approached the booth as Barnaby returned to his seat. "May I call you that?"

Patrin looked at the judge.

"Address the witness as Mr Ellis."

"I apologize, Your Honor. I was only trying to put the boy at ease. Mr Ellis, how old were you when you were at the Crusader camp?"

"About seven or eight."

"*About* seven or eight? You can't remember?"

This was what Barnaby had warned him about.

"The seasons in Australia are the opposite of what they are here in the BI," Patrin explained, "and the Crusaders never told us the date or even the month. But I remember I had my sixth birthday at home with my mam and sister before the invasion. Then while I was on the Crusader ship I began to lose track of time. After Mam found us and brought us home I had my ninth birthday. So I must have been seven and eight while the Crusaders had me."

The woman pulled a sour face. Behind her, Barnaby nodded and gave him a surreptitious thumbs-up.

The next questions the defense barrister asked went over the same incidents Barnaby had brought up. As predicted, she tried to trip him up over the details and kept her tone skeptical. He stuck like glue to what he'd already said.

It was hard. He hated thinking about those things. He hated remembering the kids who had disappeared overnight, and the cries of the ones who had been beaten. The worst images in his mind were from the night he'd escaped with Kayla, when they'd watched the barns burn in the darkness. Later on he'd learned about the kids trapped inside them.

He usually tried to blank out the memories, but the pain of going over it all again would be worth it if Seba finally paid for everything he'd done.

The old man had been found at Southern Cape, he'd heard, farming sugar cane. The locals had been suspicious about him for years. He'd continued to grow crops on the land after everyone else had taken up the new technology of using underground vats. He'd also treated his workers badly. One day police had to intervene in a vicious altercation and his picture appeared in the media. A former captive at the Australian camp had recognized him and his past caught up to him at last.

"Mr Ellis," said the barrister, "you've made serious allegations about the person you knew as Summoner Seba, but, by your own admission, you were only a young child when these events took place. Memories can be deceptive. Can you say with absolute certainty that my client is the same man who committed these acts? Isn't it possible it was someone else entirely who only bears a passing resemblance to him? Isn't that the case?"

"Your Honor," said Barnaby, "how many questions is Mr Ellis expected to answer?"

"Sustained," said the judge. "Stop badgering the witness, counsel."

"I apologize, Your Honor. Mr Ellis, how do you know for sure my client is the Summoner Seba you recall?"

"Well, he has changed a lot. He used to be fatter and he had a full head of hair…"

The woman began to smile.

"…but those jug-handle ears are unforgettable."

The roar of laughter that erupted from the audience took minutes for the judge to quieten down. In the end, he had to threaten to dismiss the public from the courtroom. Mam was wiping her eyes and TJ had his hand over his mouth as his shoulders shook.

In the general disturbance, Patrin seemed to be the only person who noticed a man rise from his seat at the back. In a flash, he ran down the aisle to the wooden barrier separating the audience from the front of the room and leapt the gate in a single bound. A guard snatched at him but missed. Someone screamed.

The man reached the defense team's desk and lifted his hand. Seba's barrister leapt out of his way, overturning her chair. Something shiny and sharp grew out of the man's hand, extending from his fist.

It was a knife.

The guard shouted at him to drop it.

But the blade swept down into Seba's neck. He did nothing to defend himself. In fact, in the few seconds of action, Seba seemed to offer up his throat.

As the knife plunged again, the guard threw himself on the stranger and wrestled him away. The blade clattered to the floor and the guard got the man down and knelt on his back. More guards arrived.

But they were too late. The damage was done.

Seba sprawled face downward in a rapidly widening pool of blood.

3

———————

"I think this is what he must have used," Wright said, sliding an interface across the dining table.

Taylan peered at the article as she took a bite of toast. It was about a new material called Flo Metal. The substance wasn't actually metal, the article explained, it only looked metallic and had several properties in common. Most importantly, it was programmable.

She lifted her eyebrows and read further.

Flo Metal could alter its shape according to digital input. As long as the total volume remained the same, it could be whatever you wanted, even things with simple working parts.

"The attacker must have brought some into the courtroom," said Wright. "The security scanners wouldn't have detected it because it isn't metal. Maybe he made it take another form so it looked like something else."

"Right. And if he had one of the new neural transmitters..."

"Exactly."

She gave a shudder, recalling the knife appearing from nothing in the man's hand and its descent into Seba's bared neck, smooth as a diver plunging into water. The blade must have been razor-sharp. She'd had a front-row seat for the murder. It had been years since she'd seen death close up and she'd grown blessedly unused to it.

Wright took the interface back. "Damned Crusaders. *All technology is evil.* Until it isn't. Bloody hypocrites."

He swiped the screen to read something else and continued to eat his bacon and eggs, shoveling the food in as if it was going out of fashion.

She smiled. Bacon and eggs must be a rare treat for a Royal Marine.

"You know you can get neural interfaces as well as transmitters now?" she asked. "No need for clunky handheld ones anymore. You could read and eat more easily."

He gave a snort of disdain. "No, thanks. *This* interferes in my life enough." He tapped behind his ear on the spot where a military comm sat beneath his skull.

She knew how he felt. She'd been relieved to have her comm removed. And she agreed with his distaste for neural interfaces. She wasn't anti-tech, but watching people interacting with something entirely invisible was creepy.

She watched him eat. Though it had been a couple of months since he'd returned from his mission, sometimes it was still hard to believe he was back. Not only had he survived the incredibly dangerous journey into deep space, he was also *here*, with her. They were together and he seemed happy about it too.

He glanced up and caught her staring. "What?"

She smiled wider and reached out to cover his hand with her own.

He grinned back, stood up, and leaned over the table to give her a bacon-flavor peck on the lips. "Are you ready? We have to leave soon."

"Ugh." She deflated. She'd been lost in the moment, forgetting today's appointment.

"Cheer up. It'll be fun."

"Fun?" she asked incredulously, then sighed. "I don't know if the kids are even awake yet. Have you seen them?"

"No, I haven't, come to think of it. Could you check? Colbourn will be pissed off if we're late."

"You say that as if I care."

Heavy footsteps descended the stairs.

"That's Patrin," Taylan said.

Her son entered, a knuckle rubbing one eye, his hair a tousled mess. He looked as though he'd barely slept.

"Bad night?" she asked.

Giving an adolescent grunt, Patrin scanned the empty plates on the table, then asked, "Is there any breakfast left?"

"There's plenty to eat in the kitchen, the same as always."

He shuffled past her.

"Don't take too long," she said to his retreating back. "We leave for the Institute for Skein Studies soon, remember?"

He didn't reply. Plates and cutlery clinked and clattered.

"Are you sure we have to take Patrin and Kayla?" Taylan asked Wright. "I don't know if it's a good idea, especially not after yesterday."

"They don't *have* to go. They're both minors. Technically, you can make the decision for them. But the Institute is expecting them, and don't you think they should know what they could be getting into?"

"I suppose you're right."

Her doubts remained.

The years that had passed since she'd returned to West BI had been peaceful and, for the most part, happy. She'd missed Wright horribly and she'd feared for his life, but getting her kids back had meant the world to her. Bringing them up had been the cherry on the cake. If it hadn't been for the absence of this gentle, intelligent, courageous man, everything would have been perfect.

Now he was back, she wanted things to stay this way. She wanted Wright to resign, to stay with her, and for them to grow old together in the usual boring, conventional manner. The Alliance's proposal made all of that impossible. As well, it put her children's lives at risk.

It was a big ask. Refusing would be perfectly reasonable. Yet on the other hand, could she, in good conscience, say no?

"Mam," Kayla called down the stairs, "I can't find my jeans."

Taylan rolled her eyes and walked into the hall. Leaning on the bannister rail, she shouted back, "Why is that my problem? Wear something else."

"I don't have anything else."

Pushing aside the mental image of Kayla's clothes-strewn room, Taylan replied, "I'm sure you can find something. Hurry up. You need to eat before we leave."

Kayla's surprised face appeared at the top of the stairs. "Where are we going?"

"You know. We talked about it last night, remember?"

"Oh, yeah. Cool." She disappeared.

Twenty minutes later, the military car had arrived and they were on their way. Kayla began telling a long, involved story about a falling out among her school friends, while Patrin stared out the car window in silence. He hadn't spoken much since yesterday and he hadn't mentioned a word about what had happened at the trial. Taylan worried about him. He was reacting exactly the same as he had to his period of captivity with the Crusaders, burying the trauma deep. She'd arranged numerous counselling and therapy sessions over the years, to no end. He simply refused to open up about his experiences or admit to any after-effects. His trial testimony had been new information.

"Hey," said Kayla, as if an idea had suddenly occurred to her, "where's Carys? Isn't she coming?"

"I invited her," Taylan replied, "but she wasn't interested. She's at the bird center."

Carys had been volunteering at the center for the rescue and rehabilitation of birds of prey for a couple of years. She loved it. It hadn't escaped Taylan's notice that her adopted daughter had gone from saving Patrin and Kayla's lives to rescuing wild animals.

"Isn't she involved in this?" Kayla asked.

"Apparently not. I told you about the mission proposal last night, remember?"

"Yeah, I remember now. Anyway, Jemima is sooo annoyed..."

Taylan faded out her daughter's prattle and rested her head on Wright's shoulder. In recognition of his exceptional service he'd been on leave since the return of the *Dauntless*. Now, after long weeks of wearing civvies, he was back in uniform, and the sight, feel, and smell of the clothes made her sad and fearful.

"Do you want to go for a walk later?" he asked quietly. "Just us?"

"I'd love to. Where do you want to go?"

He suggested a cliff-top path an hour's drive from her home. It seemed an odd destination for an evening stroll, but she agreed.

4

The Institute for Skein Studies was an imposing building. Its black marble facade rose six or so stories high—the lack of windows made it hard to be exact —and the frontage occupied the entire street. The car dropped them at the main entrance, but their instructions stated they were to go to the Mapping Department door a little further down. The single door was less imposing and the tiny sign next to it made it almost anonymous.

"Right on time," said a middle-aged woman with a long, brown ponytail who answered the buzzer. "I'm Dr Prentice. Can I check your IDs?" She added, apologetically, "It's just a formality."

Taylan waited for her to produce a scanner, but she only gazed at them expectantly.

"I, er, only need to look," Prentice explained.

She had a neural interface.

Taylan lifted her wrist to the scientist's eyes and Wright and the kids did the same.

Prentice focused on each of their embedded chips in turn. "Excellent. Nice to meet you all. Lieutenant-Colonel Wright,

Brigadier Colbourn has asked me to escort you to a separate conference room when the viewing is over."

"Okay, thanks."

"Lieutenant-Colonel?" Taylan asked as they went inside.

"I was promoted."

"You didn't say anything."

He shrugged.

Prentice led them to an elevator. They stepped in and it began to descend.

"We're going *down*?" asked Kayla.

Prentice replied, "There's less interference from living organisms underground."

"What do you mean, less interference?"

"It's complicated. You'll understand better when we show you."

Kayla pulled a face indicating she predicted utter boredom coming her way. Taylan gave a mental sigh and leaned on the elevator wall as they descended.

She watched her adolescent daughter surreptitiously as the ride continued. The Institute for Skein Studies was far more expansive below the surface and it looked like they were heading for the lowest floor, B20. Kayla's growth spurt showed no signs of slowing down. She'd always been a tall child, and now it seemed she would end up taller than her mother and perhaps nearly as tall as her towering brother. Her period of deprivation at the hands of the Crusaders didn't appear to have affected her physically and mentally she appeared unscathed too.

Thank the stars.

If only the same could be said for Patrin.

The elevator slowed and stopped and the doors opened. Prentice had indeed brought them to B20, the end of the line. It was a vast space. Hundreds of meters long and wide, the room had to extend far beneath the surrounding streets. Pillars stood at regular intervals, providing support and marking the edges of sections where workers attended banks of machinery. An electric hum and faint scent of hot plastic filled the air.

"TJ!" a voice boomed. "Taylan!"

Arthur strode toward them, and Taylan drew in a breath. The ancient king looked as strong and vital as ever, but his red-gold hair and beard had turned entirely silver-gray. However, the locks remained thick and lustrous, cascading over his shoulders and chest.

He grabbed Wright into a bear hug and landed audible thumps on his back. Then he turned to Taylan. Before she could get away, he grabbed her, too, in a suffocating hold and lifted her off her feet.

"It's good to see you too," she squeaked.

He let go, dropping her. She could breathe again.

"It's been too long," Arthur said. He turned to regard Patrin and Kayla. "And it's wonderful to see these two as well. These are the little boy and girl I saw in Australia?" Shaking his head, he added, "People have explained how much time passed on Earth while I was away, but I still find it hard to believe. Yet look at your children. Patrin is a man and Kayla is nearly old enough to be married."

"Not quite!" Taylan commented, alarmed. "Nowhere near old enough. And, strictly speaking, Patrin isn't a man yet either. He's still legally a child."

Arthur looked Patrin up and down and frowned skeptically. However, he was clearly becoming used to the oddities of this new age he found himself in, for he didn't push back on Taylan's words. Instead, he said to the boy, "Your mother told me once you love horses. Do you know how to ride?"

"No, I don't," Patrin replied. "Between school and Mam's training, I haven't had time to learn."

"Would you like me to teach you?"

"Are you kidding? I'd love it. Mam?"

"You think I'm going to make you miss out on horse-riding lessons from the King of the Britannic Isles?"

Patrin breathed a silent *Yes!*

"Excellent," said Arthur. "I believe we still have quite a while before we leave." He asked Taylan and Wright, "How do you feel about our new quest?"

"Quest?" Kayla interjected. "What's a quest?"

"A noble adventure, young maid."

"Cool. A noble adventure. I like the sound of that."

Arthur smiled. "You have your mother's brave heart, though I hope you don't have her tongue, too, for all our sakes."

"What? Why?"

"Never mind," said Taylan.

Prentice said tentatively, "Um, now you're all re-acquainted, would you mind stepping this way?" As they followed her, she continued over her shoulder, "I've been told the purpose of your visit is so I can fill you in on skein mapping. I'm not sure how much you already know."

"Personally," Wright replied, "I know very little. Arthur and I missed out on all the developments of the last few years."

"Okay, I'll start from the basics."

Heads were turning and gazes following them as they walked along the open central aisle. No doubt everyone recognized Arthur. His face had been plastered over the news media ever since the *Dauntless* had returned, but the articles Taylan had seen displayed an old photo of him. Perhaps the Alliance wanted to maintain a more youthful image of the king. The skein mappers weren't only interested in Arthur as a public figure, they also had to be as stunned as she was by his transformation.

"This is as good a spot as any," said Prentice, stopping at a quadrangle of machines. Four technicians sat in the middle facing a machine each. "Right. If I could have your attention?"

Kayla was gazing, slack-jawed at the seemingly endless rows of machinery. She returned her attention to the scientist.

"Put simply, connections exist between every living and non-living thing in the universe. We can't see them, and for a very long time we only had the smallest inkling they existed. How should I put it?" She glanced upward, brow furrowed, before continuing, "Physicists and mathematicians had spotted the signs—particles that appeared to wink in and out of existence, for instance, imaginary numbers, interactions between independent objects separated by huge distances. We understood some aspects of these things, but when we received the files from the *Dauntless*, we realized all these phenomena were like mountain tops poking up out of the ocean, indicating something hidden beneath the waves. With the help of a friendly extra-terrestrial species, we've been allowed a peek in the water."

Did she know Wright was the person the 'friendly extra-terrestrial species' had approached with the new knowledge? Clearly not, and he was the last person to blow his own trumpet.

"And what a vision it is," Prentice went on. "What a mountain-range within the ocean. Even now, years later, we haven't uncovered or applied five percent of the knowledge revealed. Yet one thing we do know with a great degree of certainty is there is a general background of connections of all matter. The Main Skein, as we like to call it. Now, you might think this would be homogenous and evenly spread out, but nothing could be further from the truth. The Main Skein has patterns and areas of density and thinness, *and* it moves. It's rippling around us as I speak. But that isn't what you're here to see today. Overlaying the Main Skein is something else. It's...well, it's easier to show you. Max?"

Apparently she wasn't abbreviating the word maximum. The man sitting nearest her nodded and his lips moved, though

Taylan didn't catch what he said. All movement in the room ceased. Seated workers' arms fell to their sides and walkers halted in their tracks.

The lights went out.

In a heartbeat, millions of lines flashed into life. Fluorescent green, they snaked from person to person, object to object, ran across the floor, and pierced the ceilings and walls at all angles. The lines ranged in thickness from mere threads to dense, brilliant bands. Thick, bright cables ran between Taylan, her children, and Wright. More bands ran from them all to Arthur.

Prentice said, "Thanks, that'll do, Max."

The lights came on and the lines winked out of existence. Except, of course, they had not. They still existed, invisible to human sight. Their traces were burning in Taylan's retinas.

"What you saw was *not* the Main Skein," Prentice said. "That's much, much more complicated and we don't have the computing power to even begin to map it yet, though we're getting there. The connections you saw was what for the moment we're calling the Secondary Skein. I doubt that name's going to last. We're starting to see divisions and layers in the Secondary Skein we'll be able to classify soon. Anyway, that's getting a bit more technical than necessary. Any questions?"

"As I understand it," said Wright, "some of these connections are pre-existing and some are created by actions. Is that correct?"

"Yes, that's one of the classifications we're working on. There's more to it, but that's the gist. We don't know enough to define the exact distinction yet."

Arthur said, "And it's this map that's leading us away from Earth again, out to—"

Prentice held up her hands to stop him. "I know what you're referring to but I can't discuss it here. My aim today is to show you the framework. You saw the connections between you all and the basic idea of the Secondary Skein. The implications of all this is something we're still working on. As far as you're concerned, you can discuss the finer details with your superiors."

"TJ," said Arthur, "what we just saw must have been what Merlin was studying the night we found Taylan in the wilderness. He must be able to see the invisible patterns."

"You mean when I was on my way back from Ynys Môn?" asked Taylan. "I always wondered how you managed that."

Wright nodded. "Merlin spent a while concentrating, then he seemed to know roughly where you were."

"But if the aliens can read the skein..." Taylan mused. She asked Prentice, "Do these lines show the future?"

The woman's features brightened in excitement, but she only said, "That's currently under investigation. I'm sorry, I don't think I can risk telling you much more. The demonstration was mostly for your children, to help their understanding."

Kayla folded her arms across her chest and a line formed between her brows, as if she felt insulted.

Taylan said, "So next it's..." She read Wright's look. "Don't tell me Colbourn's going to speak to us too."

5

———

Arthur left the elevator at the second floor above ground level, promising to be in touch to arrange horse-riding lessons with Patrin. On the tenth floor, Prentice escorted Taylan and the children to a room and asked them to wait while she took Wright somewhere else. The room was bare save for a table and a few seats. Taylan and Patrin sat down and Kayla wandered to the large wall interface. She tried to activate it, swiping the screen.

"I don't think you're supposed to do that," Taylan said.

Kayla grimaced. "It doesn't work anyway."

Taylan suspected it did work, only it didn't work for Kayla or anyone else without the proper security clearance.

"How long do we have to wait?" Kayla asked.

"I don't know. Not long, I hope."

Kayla pulled her personal screen from her pocket and after fiddling with it exclaimed, "This doesn't work either!"

"It's most likely jammed," Taylan explained. "This place must have the highest security in the country."

Kayla ambled to the clear wall separating the room from

the corridor and leaned on it, staring out morosely. "This is so *boring*," she told the glass.

"We've been here less than five minutes," Patrin said. "And the skein mapping room was pretty great."

"I suppose so, but did it really tell us anything we don't already know? Of course we're attached to each other. We're family. Except..." she turned and faced her brother "...did you notice you and the king were strongly connected? The line between you two was almost as thick as Mam and TJ's."

"I didn't notice," Patrin said. "It must be the horse-riding. I'm looking forward to that."

Taylan didn't think it could be something as inconsequential as a mutual love of horses that tied her son to Arthur. She hadn't noticed Kayla's observation and she found the news disturbing even though she didn't know what it meant.

The minutes stretched out. Brigadier Colbourn was taking her sweet time in coming to see them. Taylan guessed she had a lot to talk about with Wright. That was also disturbing. She hated the thought of him returning to service. As well as the danger involved in his job, she wasn't sure he was up to it psychologically. He hid his mental troubles well, but some things he couldn't hide from her, such as the nightmares that jolted him from sleep on a regular basis and moments of nervous distraction, when she was sure he was having flashbacks.

Every so often someone would walk past in the corridor and Kayla would unashamedly follow them with her gaze. Taylan contemplated telling her to knock it off and sit down but no one seemed bothered by the young girl's scrutiny.

A pair of workers stopped right outside their room for a chat.

"I wonder what they're talking about?" Kayla asked.

"Skein stuff," Patrin replied. "Probably things you wouldn't even understand."

"Like you *would* understand it."

"I bet I'd get it better than you. We've studied skeins at school. Just the basics, but—"

"Just because you studied it doesn't mean you understand it."

Taylan was about to tell the kids to quit bickering when the people outside concluded their chat and one of them walked away, *right through the other person.*

"Did you see that?" Kayla asked, turning, her eyes wide and mouth agape.

"She must be a holo," said Patrin.

"Has to be. I wonder how many of the people here aren't here at all. Was Dr Prentice a holo too?"

Taylan had heard rumors of holos that could move around but didn't know how they worked. Were projectors built into the fabric of the building? What feedback did the person operating as a holo receive? The encounter between the two workers had seemed entirely natural. She guessed the person who wasn't here experienced a real-time, virtual mockup of the working environment.

If only they could send holos of themselves on the mission the BA was proposing. She would agree to that in a heartbeat, but she doubted that was the case.

Colbourn appeared outside the transparent window, and Kayla drew back at the sight of the stern woman. The door slid open and the brigadier entered, all officious, no-nonsense attitude.

Didn't she ever relax? Taylan imagined the officer in a swimsuit lying on a beach sipping a cocktail, and stifled a giggle.

Colbourn shot her a murderous glance. "I am here to give you a brief summary of the Alliance's mission proposal. As civilians you are not obliged to participate, though in my opinion it would be unpatriotic, irresponsible, and undutiful for you to refuse." She bestowed another withering glare on Taylan before continuing, "Until and unless you sign a binding contract agreeing to the mission parameters, I am somewhat hamstrung about what I can tell you. However, I'll do my best."

That was it. No greeting, no introduction, no friendly small talk to put the kids at their ease.

The brigadier touched the room's interface and it lit up.

"Why wouldn't it do that for me?" Kayla whined.

The look Colbourn gave her made her shrink into the wall. Speaking between her teeth, Colbourn ordered her to sit down.

Kayla instantly did as she was told.

Taylan gave her daughter a sympathetic smile. She knew only too well how scary Colbourn was, especially to a young girl whose life had been mostly easy and comfortable.

"One thing you must understand, Ellis," the brigadier said, "If you do agree to join the mission, your children will undergo extensive training." She looked at Patrin and Kayla as if she'd just wiped them off her shoe.

Taylan clenched her hands into fists.

"Now be quiet and listen," said Colbourn.

LATER, when they'd returned home and eaten dinner, Wright reminded Taylan of their planned walk along the cliff-top path. After checking Carys wasn't going out and Patrin and Kayla wouldn't be alone, they left.

The place Wright had picked for their evening walk was one Taylan had taken him to in the early days after he'd got back from his journey into deep space. It was one of her favorite walks, though it was far from home so she didn't come here often. Small villages were the only habitations in the area, which meant the pathway was never busy. On a weekday at dusk it was predictably empty.

A stiff, cool breeze blew in and on the sea below, nearly invisible in the darkness, moonlight and starlight sparkled on foam-topped waves.

Wright's warm hand wrapped around hers, they set off along the edge of the cliff.

He didn't speak but that wasn't unusual. Wright had never been a talker. She was also quiet, thinking about the day's events.

After a while, she asked, "How do you feel about this trip? Have you made up your mind?"

"Have you?"

"I'm interested to hear what you have to say first." She bit her lip. "You know you can always resign."

"I know. I've considered it, but...I suppose we're each waiting to hear the other's decision."

"I suppose so. My biggest problem is it isn't only myself I'd be committing to the trip. I have my kids to think about too."

"So have I."

She was touched. She'd been uncertain about how Wright and her children would work out their relationships, but things seemed to be going okay.

"Let's stop here," he said.

She looked out over the dark, silver-speckled expanse, the salt-laden wind in her face. In the past, there would have been lights from container ships far out to sea. Nowadays, freight was transported underwater in huge, metal leviathans quietly powered by high-storage batteries, leaving the ocean surfaces clear of everything except leisure craft. Thanks to the scientific revelations the anonymous friends of humanity had divulged, the world was changing incredibly fast and for the better. She couldn't imagine what it would look like even five years from now.

The question that had been plaguing her ever since the Alliance had first proposed the new mission returned. Despite all she'd learned today she was no closer to a decision. There seemed to be no correct choice. But maybe there was. Maybe it was all that simple.

She sensed Wright move beside her. "Taylan."

She turned to face him only to see empty space. He had gone down on one knee.

Shocked, she took a step backward.

He grabbed her wrist. "Careful! You'll go over the edge."

"Wh-what are you doing?"

Releasing her, he reached in his pocket and took out a small box.

Her heart thumped. Everything had suddenly become surreal.

He opened the box, revealing a ring. "Taylan Ellis, will you marry me?"

There was an awkward pause.

"But...we don't need to get married."

"Yes, we do. *I* do."

"You're so traditional."

"I know. What's your answer?"

She blinked back tears. "Yes. Of course it's yes. On one condition."

6

Kala Orr studied the holo of the ship's schematics sourly. Acquiring the information had taken no end of machinations, bribery, and blackmail. In the old days, it would have been easier. Now, though she retained some power as the Dwyr it was nothing compared to the control she had once exerted. The Alliance and Prime Minister Jonte had done their work effectively during her nine years' absence from Earth, held prisoner aboard the *Dauntless*.

The place where she was forced to live was a perfect example of her reduced circumstances. She loathed the modern mansion the BI government had allotted her. She despised the boring, plain rooms and fully comprehensive range of automated services. Where was the personal touch in a laundry machine? Where was the love and awe of the arcane in a food printer? The ancient castles she had once called home had been returned to public ownership and were now filled with gawking tourists, ignorant and unappreciative of their history and atmosphere.

Lifting her lip in disgust, she returned her attention to the ghostly lines of the ship hanging in front of her. She had rarely bothered herself with technical details of the Crusade's vessels, but even to her untrained eye there was something odd about these ones. The decks, sections, weapons and engine were clearly outlined, though the engine seemed smaller than usual. All the familiar parts were here, but whoever had created the plans had differentiated between the construction materials using colors and shading. What did the differences mean?

"What's that, Mother?"

Perran.

She hastily closed the holo and snapped, "Don't sneak up on me. You gave me a fright."

"I don't think you've ever been frightened in your entire life, and I wasn't sneaking anywhere. I can't help it if you're in one of your trances. What were you looking at?"

"None of your business."

"Was it a starship?"

"I said—"

"It *was* a starship. I recognize the format. I remember recording the plan of the *Bres*."

"Oh, you do, do you? Do you also remember blabbing about arranging the explosion aboard her?"

His jaw clenched and he replied through his teeth, "I was a kid and it was Morgan's idea. How long are you going to hold that over me?"

"As long as it takes for me to return to the position I was once in. It was because of your stupid mistake I had to leave Earth for nearly a decade. If the BA hadn't been able to threaten me with exposing you—"

"We've been over this I don't know how many times! Do you have to keep reminding me? When are you going to let it go?"

She rose to her feet and stalked toward him. "You have no idea what I had to endure out there. *No* idea." The memory of Jon's ghost silently reproaching her, it seemed, for all she'd done, sprang vividly into her mind. She halted and took a breath. "No idea," she repeated, a catch in her voice.

"That's all in the past now. You need to get over it."

Dragging herself back to the present, she regarded the young man standing before her. He'd grown tall in her absence but his dark hair and dark eyes were the same. There could be no doubt he was her son. Yet she felt she hardly knew him. The BA had completed the work Morgan le Fay had begun. It had severed him from her. Perran was no longer hers. The bond was gone.

But perhaps all was not lost. Perhaps she could bind him to her again. Conceived when the Horned One came to her in the guise of many men one night in an oak grove, and born through great pain and joy, he was her blood. Nothing could change that.

The *world* was changing, however. The secrets revealed to humankind had been revelatory. The stupid scientists were finally beginning to understand the great truths of the universe, things *she* had understood and accepted for most of her life. She had been right all along. Not that anyone had given her credit for it. The Alliance's propaganda had turned the image of the Crusade into a quaint, quirky movement, its members batty but essentially harmless.

"What are you thinking, Mother?" Perran asked, looking at her strangely. "Are you feeling all right?"

"I'm fine," she retorted hotly, then, calmer, she said, "Come here and sit down." She returned to the sofa and patted it.

He joined her, looking somewhat wary.

"This trip the BA plan on taking us on," she said. "What do you think about it?"

"I think it's exciting. It's been years since I was aboard a starship."

"You do realize we'll be traveling into interstellar space, don't you? Aren't you afraid?"

"Should I be? You haven't told me much about your time on the *Dauntless*. What was it you had to endure? What made it so bad?"

"Things out there are different from how they are on Earth. Out there, there's no telling what might happen. And the *Defiant* will be heading for a new, different section of the galaxy."

"The *Defiant*?" His eyes widened. "Is that the ship's name? Was that its plans you were looking at just now? It was, wasn't it. Where did you get them?" He stood and backed away from her. "You have to destroy the files. You'll get us both in trouble."

"Sit down," she hissed, glaring.

Slowly, he complied.

It was gratifying to discover she still held sway over him. "Listen. You're my son, Perran, and for that reason and that reason alone I'll forgive you for being a sniveling, whining failure. What happened to you while I was gone? What did they do to you?"

His expression hardened, but he didn't answer.

"You weren't a small child when I left, or rather, was forced to leave. You must remember the days of the Crusade, the rites and rituals, the adoration of our followers."

"I remember," he said sullenly.

"Do you recall our time on the *Belladonna*, when Morgan taught you telepathy?"

"That was only a trick. It wasn't real." He wouldn't meet her gaze, no doubt ashamed of his betrayal when she'd tried to escape with him.

"It *was* real. Let's try now, shall we? Close your eyes and try to speak to me with your mind."

"No, it's stupid."

She put the idea to one side. For her, it had been less than a year since she'd practiced telepathy, but for Perran it had been half a lifetime ago. It was perfectly possible he'd simply forgotten how to do it.

"Another time maybe," she said. "It isn't important. Perran, I forgive you for allowing the Alliance to run roughshod over everything I worked for. You were young when I left and you were alone, lacking a guiding hand. But I'm back now. I've been back for months. Whenever I try to speak to you about how things were and how they should be, you rebuff me. You act as though everything I ever believed in, everything *we* believed in, is a nonsense. Can't you see how hurtful and disappointing that is to me?"

"I guess so," he muttered. Still, he wouldn't look at her.

"Despite everything that's happened, no matter what anyone has told you, I am your mother. Don't you think I know what's best for you?"

He shrugged.

She wasn't reaching him. She decided to try a different tactic. "Do you remember the day I attempted to launch an invasion of Ireland? The speech on the quay? Arthur's approach through the crowd?"

"How could I forget it?"

"He murdered so many of my followers in cold blood in his effort to reach me. Do you think that was right?"

"Of course not, but..." he frowned "...there was a man tied onto the front of our procession vehicle. Who was he? And why was he covered in cuts?"

Grimacing, she replied, "Sometimes, running an empire requires the performance of distasteful acts. That man was a traitor, but the people Arthur killed were innocent. Think about it. Who were the evil ones then? Us or the Alliance?"

"That was ages ago. The Britannic Isles are peaceful now. People are mostly happy."

She gritted her teeth. *Happy*? When did happiness ever count for anything?

7

———

"I can't do it!" Taylan exclaimed, "and I don't understand how you can even ask me."

Wright put his head in his hands. They had been going over and over the same topic for hours. He was sick of it. She had to be sick of it too. But he couldn't give up. It was too important. He understood her concerns but why couldn't she see his point of view? She didn't seem to want to give an inch.

When he looked up, she'd moved to the living room window and was staring out of it, her arms folded across her chest.

"You know what I went through," she murmured. Turning to face him, she continued, "You know what it did to me and how I nearly lost them. They were just kids. They've suffered enough and so have I. You saw what the trial did to Patrin. He was a mess. It's time we put it all behind us. Patrin deserves to live a happy, normal life and so does Kayla. I'm *not* dragging them into the Alliance's harebrained scheme. Everyone's acting like it isn't insanely dangerous. We'd be going up against beings vastly superior to us, with abilities and technology we can only guess at. I'm not going to subject my children to that."

She was silhouetted in the darkening room, her back to the window, so he couldn't make out her face, but her tone had risen, trembling as she spoke. She went on, "And if that means you and I have to be separated again, so be it."

There it was. That was the real point of their argument. If she didn't agree to join the mission they would be living at different speeds. While he was gone, time would pass on Earth faster than it would aboard the *Defiant*. When he returned, she could be decades older than him, or possibly dead. The physicists had said the new method of space travel, passing through seams in spacetime like areas of dead current in an ocean, meant the rules of relativity didn't apply in the same way. There would be some variance in the speed time passed but they weren't exactly sure how much.

If she didn't come with him, their relationship would essentially be over.

She said softly, "I thought I mattered to you. That we *all* mattered to you."

He gasped and strode across the room to grab her into a hug. "You do matter to me. More than I can say. You mean the world to me."

She muttered into his shoulder, limp in his arms, "But the Alliance means more."

"No!" He held her arms and looked into her eyes, shadowy in the twilight. "This isn't just another job. If it weren't for this mission I would have resigned the minute I disembarked the *Dauntless*. I was done. In fact, I was done after Jamaica. I should have left then. I'm not sure why I didn't. But I'm glad I stuck around. You said these beings we saw as Merlin and Morgan are incredibly dangerous. That's right. That's exactly why we must do something about them now, while we still can. And we can't leave it to other people to do it. It was me the aliens spoke to when they exploded our scientific understanding. That means something. Can you imagine what might have happened if it had been Arthur or Kala Orr?"

"But why did they contact you in particular? Did they explain?"

"No, but they initially tried to speak to all three of us due to the connections they saw. They first came to me looking like my father."

"Your *dad*?!"

"They seemed to pick on significant figures from our past. For Arthur it was Guinevere, and for Orr some old guy she used to know. The point is, they could see things we don't comprehend yet, even with everything they've told us. These connections are significant, and if there's a strong link between you, me, your children, and Arthur, as well as all the other links the skein mappers have discovered, it's important. I don't know how or why, but—"

"We've been over this so many times." She broke away from him. "I keep telling you I don't care. I'm not going to join the mission and I won't give permission for Patrin or Kayla to join it either. Who knows what might happen to them? I'm not putting my kids in danger. I would be a reckless, neglectful parent if I did. What you do is up to you. It would have been nice to get married, but if you insist on doing this I don't see much point. We should just try to do our best to enjoy our time together before you leave."

"Taylan, I don't want to leave without you." He wasn't sure he even could. Looking at her standing before him, he imagined the wrench it would be to tear himself from her side. The experience on the *Dauntless* had been terrible. He didn't know if he could do it again. Yet if he didn't, he wasn't sure how it might impact the future of humanity.

In a way, he wished he could see things through her narrow, focused scope, but he couldn't.

"You realize you could still be jeopardizing your children's future?" He felt bad hitting her below the belt but he didn't see any alternative.

"Huh? By refusing to allow them to travel into unknown danger?" she asked icily. "Explain that."

He hesitated. There was so little he could tell her. "We have free will. That's clear. Some connections are formed by our actions. But there's also a natural passage of things—the map indicates it. The alien told me the *Dauntless* was smashing through the web of connections, that there were easier and less destructive routes to take. If we—you—don't follow the indications, no one knows what might happen."

"No one knows what'll happen if I do!"

"We're currently heading for a better world for all humankind, right? But what if Merlin and Morgan return soon? They don't give a shit about us. We're like ants to them. What do you think Earth will be like for Patrin and Kayla then, and their children's world? We have to try to put a stop to their interference. Our new knowledge of the skeins seems to give us a chance, but only if we put it to use. Otherwise, we remain ignorant, barely sentient beings, smashing through the spider's silk wherever we go."

"That's hypothetical. You're trying to scare me, and it isn't fair."

"What choice do I have when you won't listen to reason?"

"I'm not the one being unreasonable here."

"But you are! Weren't you there at the Institute with me? Didn't you see the patterns?"

"I saw a lot of pretty lights, yes. That doesn't mean I have to pay attention to them."

"Now look," said Wright, his ire rising. "You're being disingenuous. It was the connections that led you to your kids out in Australia. It was all due to what Arthur told you about recognizing the pattern. You didn't believe him at first but in the end you had to admit he was right. That's what you told me."

She was silent.

"If it wasn't for you following the connections, Patrin and Kayla would have died in the desert. That's true, isn't it?"

Still, she didn't reply.

"Answer me."

"I want you to leave," she said quietly.

"What?"

"I want you to go. Now. Take what you need for tonight. When you know your new address I'll send the rest of your stuff on."

He stared at her. "Come on, Taylan. You're being ridiculous. We're just having a discussion."

"Take your things," she hissed, "and get out!"

He froze, watching her, trying to figure out what was going on. How had their argument suddenly transformed into a break-up? It was the last thing he wanted.

The door chime sounded.

Kayla's footsteps resounded from the staircase as she bounded down. She had a thing about answering the front door. It hadn't been by chance it had been Kayla who opened it when Wright had arrived at Taylan's house two months ago, when he'd desperately hoped she still loved him. Could everything really be over?

"Uncle Lorcan!" came Kayla's happy voice from the hall. "It's been ages. Come in."

The hall light turned on and Kayla stuck her head into the living room. "Uncle Lorcan's here." Quizzically, she continued, "Why are you standing in the dark?" She turned on the light and returned to the hall.

"*Uncle Lorcan*?" Wright asked.

He could see Taylan's face properly now, including the tracks of tears on her cheeks. He felt an absolute bastard.

She wiped her face with the cuff of her shirt. "Yes, it's Ua

Talman. He comes around sometimes. We haven't seen him for a while, not since you got back."

The man himself stepped into the living room. His trademark red hair had turned white and he was stooped and frail-looking. The years of the *Dauntless's* voyage had passed heavily for him. "Good evening, Taylan. Ah, I recognize your other visitor. It's Major Wright, isn't it? I remember you."

Not bothering to offer an update on his rank, Wright shook Talman's offered hand. "You have a good memory. I have to confess I didn't expect to see you here."

Kayla had skipped to the liquor cabinet and was pouring whiskey into a tumbler.

"I pop in now and then," said Talman. "I like to check how Patrin and Kayla are doing and it's nice to have a touch of normality once in a while."

"Do you want to sit outside on the patio?" Kayla asked. "It's a beautiful evening."

"That's a very good idea. It is indeed a lovely evening. Perhaps you two would like to join me for a small tipple?" he asked Taylan and Wright, glancing from one to the other as if sensing the tension between them.

"I will," Taylan replied. "In a minute. Wright's just about to leave."

"I'm sorry to hear it. I would have liked a chat. Perhaps he could stay a short while and indulge an old man?" He was asking Taylan.

"All right," she replied sullenly. "If you like."

Talman followed Kayla out of the living room, heading for the back of the house.

Wright was entirely nonplussed, trying to wrap his head around the fact that the richest man in the world was in Taylan's home.

She seemed to guess his confusion. "Lorcan started dropping by not long after the *Dauntless* left. He would talk to the kids about how they were getting on, ask to see their school reports, things like that. I think he guessed I was a single mum and he was trying to be a father figure to them. Seeing them seemed to help him, too, in some way, though I'm not sure. He never explained why he was here. But over time the kids have grown to love him."

"They're very lucky."

"I know. And," she added, her tone hardening, "I want them to stay that way."

Outside, the sun had set and the back garden was warm and peaceful. Small bats swooped through the dusky sky, gathering flying insects.

Ua Talman sat at the patio table, his tumbler in hand, quietly talking to Kayla. "Ah, Wright. Glad you could stay. But neither of you has a drink."

"I'll get them," Kayla piped. "What do you want?"

When they gave their answer she trotted into the house.

Wright pulled out a slatted seat and sat down. The end of the garden was only just visible. He recalled seeing Taylan there for the first time in nine years, sparring with Patrin. He'd thought the nearly fully grown boy was Taylan's new man and had been so relieved to discover he wasn't.

He hadn't imagined this final mission would drive them apart after such a short time together. In an attempt to distract himself from his pain, he said to Lorcan, "When I got back, I was surprised to find out your colony ships were still here. Weren't they supposed to leave years ago?"

The man had sipped his whiskey. He sucked in a breath through thinned lips before replying, "They were, but when the scientific revelations arrived, I realized I couldn't allow the colonization project to go ahead as it was. We've worked through everything again, right from the basics up. We had to strip the ships down to their frames and rebuild them."

"That must have been a massive effort."

"Massive and extremely time-consuming. Hence the years of delay. But if a thing's worth doing it's worth doing well. Though we've lost time now, we'll more than make up for it on the outward journey." He smiled. "Not that all the prospective colonists understand. And some have died waiting, unfortunately. We've had to hand out plenty of refunds. But there are always people ready and waiting to take the empty spots."

Kayla returned and handed Taylan a glass of wine and another tumbler of whiskey to Wright.

"Are you still going?" Wright asked. Ua Talman's project had been his life for decades. It had seemed the main reason for his existence.

"Perhaps not. I'm an old man. As time has worn on, my passion has faded, and I have no interest in the stars and other planets anymore. The point of what I was doing got lost along the way. Somehow, I've learned contentment." He turned his attention from the shadowy garden to Wright and Taylan. "But don't let my experience put you two off. The Alliance doesn't let me in on many of their secrets these days, but I know about the *Defiant*. The trip sounds very exciting."

Taylan remained stubbornly silent.

"Probably more challenging than exciting," said Wright. "The voyage on the *Dauntless* was no joke. But I believe it's necessary."

"You have my best wishes for success, though I doubt I'll still be alive when you return." He added, pointedly, "You'll have each other, that's the main thing. You're very fortunate. I wish I'd had longer with Grace and my children. Alas, it was not to be. If I were to give one piece of unsolicited advice to young couples it would be to cherish what you have. You never know when it'll be taken away from you."

❧

With a heavy heart, Wright stepped over the threshold of the hotel. His ID had been read by the scanner built into the wall. The hotel was one of those fully automated places with no human staff on site. A holo map of the building's layout appeared in the lobby, the empty rooms highlighted. If he had a neural net the image would have appeared only in his vision. He figured out the nearest available room and headed for it.

He hadn't brought any of his things from Taylan's home. He didn't need anything for tonight and he could buy whatever he needed. He'd left nothing sentimental there. He didn't have anything sentimental.

The door opened at his touch. From now until he checked out, it wouldn't open for anyone else except for hotel staff. The innovations were piling up, one upon the other. What would the world look like when he returned?

He wondered what the Crusaders had made of all the changes.

After quickly showering, he climbed between the cold sheets. Some things never changed. Hotels were as soulless and anonymous as always.

Sleep usually came quickly to him, but this night was different. He lay painfully awake for hours, ruminating. He'd tried everything he could think of but he couldn't seem to get through to Taylan. At the end of the day it was her decision. She couldn't be compelled to join the mission, and Kayla and Patrin were minors. She had the final say on her children's inclusion. Patrin would turn eighteen this year but his birthday fell after the scheduled departure date.

Finally, with Taylan's averted, tear-streaked face in his mind's eye, he must have fallen asleep, for something was waking him up.

At first, he thought it was his comm and he mentally answered it, but then he realized the bleeping sound was external. He opened his eyes on darkness, lit by the flashing of the room's interface. It was still nighttime. He must have only been asleep a short while.

He opened the screen but the caller was using only audio, not video.

"Wright?"

The speaker's voice was thick with long crying and sorrow, but it was unmistakable.

"Taylan? Are you okay?"

"I was wrong. I'm sorry."

"What?"

"I hate the thought of putting Kayla and Patrin in danger, but you were right about how Arthur helped me find them. What he said about patterns turned out to be true. I changed my mind. We'll come on the mission."

He sat up. "You will? You're sure?"

"I'm sure. I was only scared about what might happen to the kids. It's my job to protect them."

"I know. I get it. I really do. But if you'll come, that's fantastic."

"We will." A pause. "I love you."

"I love you too."

There was another pause, then Taylan said, "Wright?"

"Yes?"

"Come home."

8

The skein mappers had been busy. Hans scanned the list of names they'd sent him. Each person was supposedly connected to the alien invasion of human society. *How* they were connected, *why* they were involved, no one could say, only that a band of mysterious origin ran, thick and true, between these people.

Not all of the names on the list were even BI citizens. Several were from Australia, one was from St. Kitts and another was from Hawaii. How could they possibly be associated?

Probably, if a researcher investigated their backgrounds, links would be found. In his years in espionage, he'd often stumbled across unlikely relationships between subjects—relationships of which they were entirely unaware: CEOs who were distant cousins of families their corporations were screwing over; an assassin tasked with the murder of his grandmother's first love; a spy bleeding state secrets from the daughter of a woman his brother dallied with in a holiday romance decades ago.

Connections, connections, connections.

His career had been built on them, and now it seemed the

fate of humanity rested on them too. Were humans ever to be vulnerable to interference from more developed species, or could they achieve true autonomy? And if so, how?

The answer seemed to lie in the list on the screen but its significance was as opaque to him as it was to everyone else. It was not a position he liked to be in. His confidence and comfort lay in being one step ahead of his opponents. But this was something different. This was an act of faith. He would have to let go and trust the process.

Word had come through that Taylan Ellis was on board, so that was something. She was highly skilled and resourceful, though she had a knack for getting herself and others—including him—into trouble. His sources told him she was in a romantic relationship with Lieutenant-Colonel Wright, another mission member. His feelings about Wright were not so sanguine. The BA thought highly of the man but in Hans's personal experience he was unreliable.

It couldn't be helped. Like the unfathomable pattern they had chosen to follow, including Wright was something he had to do on faith. Plus, Taylan wouldn't want to leave him behind as who knew how long the *Defiant* would be gone? The same applied to her children. He was uncomfortable about sending minors out into deep space.

"Sir," said his secretary over his desk comm, "you have five minutes until your press conference."

"Thank you."

He rose and walked to his private restroom, where he washed his hands and face. It was a ritual he'd developed over the years of his rise to Prime Minister. The familiar actions centered him, concentrating his focus. Journalists and their questions were the bane of his career but they were a necessary evil.

His ritual helped him marshal his thoughts and anticipate the difficult answers he might have to give, but it was also a reminder of a moment over a decade ago when he had checked his appearance before attending the General Council meeting in Jamaica. The bombing of the event by the combined EAC and Antarctic Project forces had been a watershed. Josephine, his PA at the time, had saved his life and in doing so lost her own. That action had allowed her twin sister, Mariya, to step into her place. Mariya, who with her beguiling charms had helped him engineer a military coup of the BI Government. Mariya, a secret agent of the EAC, who had alerted Kala Orr to the Alliance's vulnerability. Mariya, his only true love, who had died a revolutionary.

Though she had subjected him to terrible torture, he hoped he was a better person for having known her. He didn't think he had played so fast and loose with people's lives since then.

The evidence of his work was all around. The Caribbean had its independence at last, the Britannic Isles was a peaceful, prosperous country, more or less united, and the Earth Awareness Crusade had diminished to largely powerless group of people with rather odd beliefs. The last he'd heard, the cult was hemorrhaging followers, particularly younger members who had attended regular state schools.

Kala Orr still lived, unfortunately, protected only by her significance to humanity's involvement with the aliens, according to the skein mappers. Perhaps it was for the best. If executed for her many war crimes she would become a martyr to her people, increasing their religious fervor and perhaps sparking a resurgence of the dangerous movement.

He had achieved many things, subtly or overtly. His dream of a BI republic had come true in all but name. Soon, King Arthur would leave on another long voyage. Who knew when he would return, if ever? Hopefully, by the time he was back, the citizens of the Isles would inform him he was no longer needed.

Hans doubted he would receive any acclaim for what he

had done. These days, all he heard were complaints and criticisms. Such was the fate of those burdened with profound responsibilities. The fact didn't particularly bother him. History, not the general public, would be his judge. To fulfill his deepest ambition was enough of a reward.

He gazed into the mirror. His beard was graying and lines surrounded his sagging eyes.

Yes, he had reward enough. Only...

There was a knock at the door.

"Sorry to disturb you, sir, but the press are waiting. Should I tell them you've had an unexpected delay?"

"No, I'll be out in a moment."

Had five minutes passed so quickly?

He took a final look in the mirror.

He *was* content with everything he'd achieved, only it would have been nice if Mariya had been by his side.

9

———

"The Prime Minister's giving a speech!" Kayla called from downstairs.

Patrin ignored her. Kayla was always getting excited about one thing or another. This time, it wasn't the Prime Minister speaking to the media that interested her, it was because Mam had told them she knew Jonte during the war. They'd done some stuff together, apparently, though she hadn't explained exactly what.

She hadn't been lying. Patrin was sure about that. Mam didn't lie or even exaggerate. If she said she'd known Jonte it was true, but she didn't know him anymore. He wasn't like Uncle Lorcan, who turned up every month or so to check how they were doing, sometimes bringing them a cool present. The PM was just another public figure. He and Mam had nothing to do with each other.

He picked up his gloves and went downstairs.

"Are you going out?" Kayla asked from the living room, spying him through the open door.

"I go out this exact same time every week," he replied, exasperated. "You know why."

"Oh, yeah. Hey, come and listen to this. It's about us."

"Huh?" He stepped into the room.

The Prime Minister stood behind a polished wooden lectern on a raised dais in front of his residence. The camera angle took in the tops of the heads of reporters clustered tightly around him, jostling for their positions.

Jonte appeared to be answering a question. "I am not at liberty to discuss the selection criteria, but suffice to say only the very best candidates, most suited to enduring the rigorous challenges of the mission, will be invited to participate."

Someone asked, "Can anyone apply?"

"Absolutely not. Individuals have already been approached on a person-by-person basis."

"But it isn't only military personnel who will be going?" the same journalist urged.

"A range of people from all walks of life have been chosen to represent humanity on this expedition, after an intensive consultation process with our heads of armed forces and scientists working at the forefront of our new understanding."

Patrin asked, "He's going public about the *Defiant*?"

"He hasn't mentioned her by name yet," Kayla replied. "The press seem more interested in who's going, not what ship they'll be aboard." She clasped her hands together. "I *wish* I could tell my friends. Keeping it a secret is killing me!"

"Don't you dare. You'll spoil everything. And then they might not let us go. Besides, your friends could all be grown up by the time we get back. Remember what happened with Mam and TJ? He was gone for nine years and she had to wait for him."

"I know. It's sooo romantic," Kayla gushed. "And now they're getting married. I can't wait for the wedding."

"I can. I'm terrified about being best man."

"Don't be stupid. It'll be awesome. My bridesmaid's dress is beautiful."

Jonte had continued his speech while they chatted. As they returned their attention to the screen, he said, "I'm afraid that's all I have time for today. It's been a pleasure to talk to you about this jewel in the crown of the Alliance's achievements. I'm sure you'll join me in wishing the men and women the very best of luck in this monumental endeavor." Ignoring questions shouted from the audience, Jonte stepped down from the podium.

Patrin frowned. "Did he say anything about the alien threat?"

"Nope, didn't mention it at all. He probably doesn't want to scare people."

It seemed unfair that the PM hadn't talked about the real reason for the mission. He appeared to be spinning it as an exploratory journey into the unknown, talking up the exciting part and downplaying the risks. Jonte was a typical politician. Patrin wasn't sad Mam no longer had anything to do with him.

He said goodbye to Kayla and left.

THE SET UP at the riding stables was always the same. Three black limousines sat outside, professional drivers at their controls, and men and women in dark suits and sunglasses hovered around the entrance.

Patrin didn't know how Arthur put up with his ever-present retinue. It would annoy the hell out of *him* to be constantly followed, with never a moment of privacy until you were behind a locked door. Even then, guards would be posted outside 24/7. Was Arthur's home fitted with cameras and listening devices too?

Mam had explained it was all because his life was under constant threat from Crusader extremists. The nutcases believed the king had pushed Kala Orr to one side, making her a powerless figurehead. In fact, Mam said, it was the Alliance who had done that and Arthur was just as much a figurehead as Orr, but it suited the BA to allow the king to be a scapegoat.

He walked up to the entrance and sighed as he lifted his arms. The security agents had to recognize him on sight by now, but they still searched him thoroughly every time he arrived for a lesson.

"Good morning, Mr Ellis," said a bald-headed man. He ran his gaze up and down Patrin, gently turned him around, and then said, "Nothing like the old methods." He patted Patrin's legs, felt up his back and sides and into his jacket collar, then turned him around again. The thorough search continued until the man felt the lump in his jacket pocket and took out the gloves. After inspecting them thoroughly, he handed them back. "You can go in. Have a good lesson, kid."

The literal rite of passage over, Patrin walked through the gates.

Arthur was already in the cobbled stable yard, holding the reins of two big stallions. The horses had to be large to comfortably carry his and Arthur's weight. Arthur's mount was the bay he always rode, but Patrin didn't recognize the other one, a dapple gray.

"Who's this?" he asked, reaching out to pat the animal's neck.

The horse backed off as if startled, his hooves clattering on the cobbles.

"Whoa," said Arthur. "Easy." He had a tight grip on the reins and brought the horse forward again. "This is Beamer."

"Like the gun?" Patrin appraised the horse. He was beautiful but his muscles twitched with tension.

"Ah yes, that's what the name means. Justin isn't available today. He's pulled a muscle. The only other horse suitable for you is Beamer. Though..." he squinted over his shoulder "...he's a little excitable."

"Just a little," Patrin said, catching a flash of white in the horse's eyes.

"I can ride him instead," Arthur offered.

"No, it's okay. I'm sure he'll settle down once we're out on the trail. He probably doesn't get ridden much so he's full of energy." He took the reins from Arthur and led Beamer the few paces to the mounting block.

Once in the saddle, the usual sense of familiarity washed over him. He never felt as at home anywhere as he did on a horse's back. He didn't understand it and couldn't explain it, except that the animals had held a fascination for him all his life. The cart horses at the Crusaders' camp in the Australian desert had been about the only positive thing in his life at the time. After his first lesson, Arthur had told him he was a natural and they hadn't ridden in the training ring since the first day.

"You lead," said the king. "I'll follow."

Patrin picked one of the many tracks leading from the stables, one that wound up a wooded slope until it reached an expanse of grassland at the top. No other riders were around. None were allowed while Arthur was present.

Patrin gave Beamer a light kick and guided him to the trail head. Soon, they were in cool shade beneath the trees' canopy and his horse was picking his way delicately over roots snaking across the track. Patrin leaned forward as the incline increased and his horse climbed upward, dealing with the extra effort with ease. After fifteen minutes' riding, they were at the top and broke out into bright sunlight.

The tree line continued to their left. On their right, tall grasses undulated in the breeze. Arthur urged his horse forward until they were riding abreast. Unusually for the situation, the king's head was down and he held his reins listlessly.

"Is something wrong?" Patrin asked. All their previous rides had seemed to invigorate him. Patrin had thought he'd never seen a man so much in his element.

Without looking at him, Arthur replied, "I have watched you ride many times now and I have formed an impression I cannot shake. It saddens me."

"What kind of impression? Am I doing something wrong?"

Arthur murmured, "You are your mother's son, and there's nothing I can do about it."

"But...why is that bad?"

As Patrin spoke, crashes resounded from the forest, like several things dropping to the floor and smashing into the brambles and bracken. Before Arthur could answer, a figure sprang from under the cover of the trees and sprinted toward them.

A flash of light erupted from his hand. He was firing!

Where was the security detail?

They couldn't gallop out of danger. Though the attacker was on foot, a pulse round could hit Arthur in the back. Patrin brought Beamer around, tugging hard on the reins, to put himself and his horse between Arthur and the would-be assassin.

Another light flashed, somewhere in the woods. More than one cultist must have dropped from the trees and now the security agents were in battle with them, but no one was protecting Arthur. Patrin was an expert with many weapons thanks to Mam's teaching but he had nothing with him.

He kicked Beamer again and rode directly at the Crusader.

All his horse's skittishness was gone. Neck outstretched, the animal bore down on the black-clothed figure like a torpedo locked on its target.

The man fired again, aiming around Patrin, and the pulse flew past so close it nearly blinded him with its glare. No sound came from Arthur so he assumed the round missed its target.

The assassin wavered, his attention flicking from the horse

and rider set on a direct course for him and a spot behind them, presumably Arthur. His arm moved fractionally right. Now he was aiming at Patrin, who was so close he could see the gun's opening, the small black hole through which would pass the bolt of concentrated energy that would be his death.

Even if his resolve had wavered, he had no choice now except to continue on his course. Beamer would not be able to deviate from his path in time to avoid the shot. No horse could. But Patrin didn't want to turn aside anyway. The resolve had gripped him like he'd never felt before. He would protect Arthur even at the cost of his own life.

A pulse flashed right before his eyes.

His vision turned red. He couldn't see a thing.

He felt Beamer leap lightly, carrying him upward, and then he landed—softly for a horse his size. His gait slowed.

Patrin drew on the reins, blinking. He had to stop his mount from running in among the trees where, judging from the hiss of pulse fire and the cracking of twigs, the battle between cultists and security agents continued.

His sight began to return, the tall green grasses and brown tree trunks swimming into view.

"That was noble and brave of you," said Arthur. The king was by his side.

Patrin looked back to the spot where Beamer had spontaneously jumped. In a patch of flattened grass lay the body of the Crusader, his chest collapsed into a charred, smoking hole.

Confused, Patrin looked at Arthur again and this time noticed he was holding a gun.

"I've been practicing with this lately," said the king, lifting the weapon. "That was a good shot, don't you think?"

Patrin swallowed. "Yes, a very good shot."

Arthur leaned closer, rising up in his stirrups, before saying conspiratorially, "We'd better not mention this to your mother."

10

—————

"How very Hans," Taylan remarked.

The PM had arranged a farewell ceremony for the mission members—along with a publicity shoot. The men and women soon to board the *Defiant* stood in a line outside the shuttle that would fly them to the ship, surrounded by press reps. Jonte walked slowly along the line, shaking each person's hand and chatting with them briefly before moving on.

The ceremony had been marketed as being about the people embarking on the voyage into deep space, traveling farther than any human had ever been. It was supposed to be a public thank you for their sacrifice, putting their lives on the line, postponing their futures.

But of course it was all propaganda. The intention was to make Hans look humble yet powerful and to polish the BI government's image. Once the *Defiant* had departed the mission would be quickly forgotten, no longer the news of the day. Comms from the ship would arrive instantly on Earth but at the speed she traveled they would be years and possibly even decades apart. It all depended on how far the *Defiant* had to go before the anticipated encounter with the extra-terrestrial life forms.

The skein mappers had been vague about her final destination. They had some idea about where the connections from Earth into outer space converged but the region discovered so far was vast, light years across. They'd said they would have a better idea as time went on, and they would comm the ship with more exact coordinates. But there was no guarantee they would ever pinpoint it exactly.

"Taylan."

The PM had arrived.

"Hans." She smiled wickedly, winding him up by using his first name when everyone else had called him Prime Minister or Sir.

He smiled back. He knew what she was doing and didn't mind. She liked that about him. He had no airs or graces. "I'm sorry we didn't get to spend more time together after your return from Australia. Unfortunately, the demands of public office—"

"I understand. I would have liked to see you too, but you were busy rebuilding the BI. That was an important job and you've done it well."

"Thank you. That means a lot to me, coming from you. You always speak your mind."

"Some wouldn't put it so politely, but you're right. If I didn't mean it I wouldn't say it."

"Good luck, Taylan. When you return, come and see me. I'll make time. It's been an honor to know you." He shook her hand firmly, then he moved on.

She reeled from his compliment. Considering she'd nearly got him hanged the praise was unexpected. But perhaps he didn't really mean it. In some ways he was her polar opposite. He'd probably never spoken his mind in his entire life.

It didn't matter. She took a last look at Jonte's profile and then stared into the distance, waiting for the ceremony to be over.

She'd seen some familiar faces as the mission members arrived and was itching to say hi to some of them. Not all, but most. It was the first time most of the team was together. The motley group was to form the core of the enterprise, supported by Royal Marines, skein advisors, and auxiliary staff. They comprised the people whose connections were tightly woven, like the core of a spider's web.

Most of them wore the mission uniform, navy blue with gold trimming. Taylan's was uncomfortably tight and hot. It was horrible to be in uniform again.

The gray airfield baked under the hot afternoon sun, entirely empty to the fields at its edge. All aircraft except for the shuttle were in the hangars and the skies had been made a no-fly zone. Crusader attacks had ramped up recently, possibly in response to the Dwyr's imminent departure.

She and her loathsome son were two of the few not present. They would have no public farewell. Hans's spin doctors had made up a lie about her being unwell and Perran unwilling to leave her side. Both had been transported directly to the *Defiant* yesterday.

Taylan looked to the side.

Hans had nearly reached the end of the line.

Thank the stars.

She risked reaching for Wright's hand now the two of them were out of close scrutiny. He frowned at her, no doubt disapproving the break in acceptable behavior, but he didn't pull his hand away as she lightly held his fingertips.

The Prime Minister posed for some more shots with the mission team in the background, and then the ordeal was finally over. As he climbed into his limousine Taylan slumped in relief. They were waved onto the shuttle and the media closed in to gather more images for the world's news agencies.

"Lieutenant-Colonel Wright!" a voice shouted from the crowd. "Is it true you and another mission member got married recently?"

Wright ignored the speaker, but Taylan looked over her shoulder. The reporter, a young woman, noticed her behavior and pushed forward. "Are you Mrs Wright? How do you feel about taking part in the mission? Is that why you were chosen? Because you're the Lieutenant-Colonel's wife?"

They were forbidden from speaking to the press in any way, shape, or form. Otherwise, Taylan might have given the woman a piece of her mind. But the question showed how ignorant the world's population was of what was really going on. They had no idea about how the skeins worked or their significance.

"Come on," Wright muttered. "Get aboard before they ask any more stupid questions."

She took a final look at the scene around the shuttle: the plain, hot, empty airfield, the mob of gawking reporters, distant yellowing grass, and crystal clear blue sky. It was her last vision of Earth for who knew how long.

Patrin walked ahead of her into the passenger cabin closely followed by Kayla. He picked a row of four seats and they all sat down, Taylan in an aisle seat.

The trip had finally begun.

"Hey, it's good to see you again," said a young man sitting down across from her.

"Kevin!" She reached out and gripped his hand. "Damn, it's good to see you too." She was forced to let go of him to allow the other passengers to pass by. "I remember you saying you didn't want to visit the Isles. Bet you never thought you'd be here, let alone boarding a flight to a starship."

"It's hotter than I thought it would be."

"We do have the occasional warm day." She couldn't stop grinning at him.

"Where's Arthur?" Kevin asked. "I thought he was coming too."

"He has his own farewell ceremony. We'll see him tomorrow."

"Yeah, while I remember, thanks for not telling me he was the freaking King of the Britannic Isles. I wouldn't have let him ride my motorbike if I'd known."

"No problem. Arthur prefers it when people don't recognize him. He hates all the deference and special treatment. Oh." She'd just spotted a line of four approaching up the aisle. Re-acquainting herself with these people would be less pleasant.

"Taylan." Meilyr passed by.

Madog was next. He nodded at her. Medwyn moved past as if she didn't exist. Marc bent down for a quick hug and whispered, "Talk later."

A woman followed him, the last to board the shuttle.

"Remember me?" she asked.

"Seren! As if I could forget. I thought I would never see you again."

Seren had aged a little but she looked as sweet and pretty as ever. Anyone who didn't know her would never guess she'd been a linchpin in the BI Resistance.

"To be honest," Seren said, "I don't know why I'm here. I was asked to come along but no one has explained why."

"I don't think the organizers know much more than we do, but I'm glad you came."

"I had to. It was either that or split up with Marc and neither of us wanted that."

"Please take your seats," a voice announced over the intercom.

But the shuttle didn't take off right away. Colbourn appeared from the pilot's cabin.

"Good afternoon, everyone. For those of you who haven't met me yet, I am Brigadier Colbourn, one of the officers in charge of this mission. I am the conduit between the civilian and military sections of the crew and your port of call regarding any problems in this area. However, be aware I value my time and I won't waste it on spurious nonsense." Her disdain for everything and everyone non-military was almost palpable.

"I am also the person who will provide you with mission updates. I am here to announce there has been a slight change of plan. We will be arriving at the *Defiant* in four hours as scheduled, but we will not be departing the Solar System directly. The ship will dock at Mars Station for upgrades and to pick up the remaining mission members. That is all. Please prepare for takeoff."

11

The cool, filtered air of a starship washed over Taylan as she boarded the *Defiant,* the unique scent evoking powerful emotions. She associated being aboard a space-faring vessel with being separated from her kids, never knowing if she would see them again or if they were even alive. They were right here, beside her, but despair and fear welled up, and she reached out to touch them.

"Mam, are you okay?" Patrin asked.

Wright, perhaps misinterpreting her expression for regret, put an arm around her. "You made the right decision. I'm sure of it."

Then his arm slid away as he saluted.

Colbourn returned the salute. "Welcome aboard, Lieutenant-Colonel."

"Thank you, ma'am."

The brigadier ran an icy stare over Taylan, Patrin, and Kayla before stalking off without saying a word to them.

"Why does that old woman hate us?" Kayla asked, long before Colbourn was out of hearing range.

Colbourn's back stiffened but she didn't break stride.

"Shhh," said Wright. "Brigadier Colbourn is a Royal Marine officer. She deserves our respect."

"No, she doesn't," said Taylan. "Kayla, she hates us because she's a bitter old witch, not because we did anything wrong."

"Taylan!" Wright admonished.

"It's true." She continued to her daughter, "She hates almost everyone except Wright. Don't take it personally."

"Okay," Kayla blithely replied. "Where's my cabin? This is so exciting." She had gathered her duffle bag into her arms and was squeezing it to her chest.

The packing of the bag had been a prolonged, complicated exercise, involving many complaints and hard decisions about what to bring and what to leave behind. The volume and weight restriction for luggage applied to all mission members equally, regardless of the size of their wardrobe. In the end Taylan had given Kayla half the space in her own bag just to get her to shut up.

"Sir," said a young Marine, approaching them. "I am to show you to your quarters."

The *Defiant* was a sleek vessel. There was no denying it. As well as the familiar but disturbing scent of a starship, the air held notes of newness: fresh paint, metal vapors of solder fumes, antiseptic odors from the sanitizing sweep before she was cleared for boarding. But there was something else about her that felt strange.

Taylan had served aboard several military vessels, from the corvette, the *Daisy*, to the fleet's flagship, the *Fearless*. Each ship had been different yet in some ways they were the same. The doorways had all been arched. The passageways had been identical in cross-section: a square with the edges cut off. The bulkheads had been smooth except for the indentations for hand—

"Where are the little bars for holding onto in case we lose gravity?" she asked.

The Marine replied, "No need for them, ma'am."

"What do you mean, there's no need? We're in space."

"It's impossible for the *Defiant* to lose gravity. That can only happen if the ship disintegrates, when we'll have more problems than not knowing which way is up."

"Huh?" Taylan turned her puzzled expression to Wright.

"I don't understand it properly either," he said. "It's something to do with the new engineering. Gravity is part of the fabric of space within the ship. It's a part of her design."

"Right," said Taylan, though she was no closer to comprehending.

"What?" Kayla asked, outraged. "You mean I did all that zero-gravity training for nothing? I threw up a million times!"

The Marine grinned. "Sorry about that, miss. You might be interested to hear another aspect of the *Defiant's* design. She's partly organic."

"Organic? You mean flesh and blood?"

"Living material helps her move through the skein." He gave an embarrassed grin. "I don't claim to know exactly what that means. That's just what the scientists and engineers say. All of this is top secret, of course. That's why you couldn't know these things until you came aboard."

"Then how come you're telling us now?"

When the young man didn't answer, Taylan said, "Because by the time we get back it won't be."

"Oh," Kayla said, her expression troubled.

Was she only just beginning to understand that years would pass on Earth while they were gone? The fact had been made plain to her several times over the last few months but she was barely a teenager. Her mind was on many things but physics wasn't one of them. For her, the here and now were all that was important and she probably didn't think about much else.

The uncomfortable realization was quickly forgotten when Kayla saw her cabin. Space was tight on the starship, but in recognition of their non-military and minor status she and Patrin had been given singles. Taylan and Wright shared a double between them. She left the kids to settle into their new homes while she and Wright unpacked. The orderliness with which he folded and stored his possessions was mildly disturbing, but military life was all he'd known since he was eighteen. She guessed some things about him would never change. She stowed her few belongings.

Next came yet another briefing, this time in the vessel's small auditorium.

"Surely they've told us everything there is to know?" she asked as they took seats.

"Like the Marine said," Wright replied, "we're aboard ship now. We can't comm Earth, so we're effectively cut off from everyone except our shipmates. This is where we hear the stuff they couldn't or didn't want to tell us before."

They were among the last to arrive. As soon as they were seated, a short man in Royal Navy uniform walked to the front of the room.

"Who's that?" Taylan whispered. "He looks familiar."

After a quiet sigh that told her she should already know the answer to her question, Wright replied, "Admiral of the Fleet, Yorkson."

"Was he the one on the *Fearless* that Merlin brought back to his senses?"

"That's right. I'm surprised it's him, not Lieutenant-General Carol, leading the mission. We have to be quiet now."

The admiral seemed about to speak but conversational buzz in the room continued. He frowned. He probably wasn't used to addressing civilians, who wouldn't give him his accustomed deference and instant obedience. It took him loudly clearing his throat to make everyone pipe down.

"Ladies and gentlemen, officers, and Marines, it gives me great pleasure to welcome you aboard the *Defiant*. While many of you are under orders and therefore have no choice about being here, a significant proportion of you are not. You have chosen to join this mission and leave behind your lives on Earth of your own free will, and for that you have my and the BI Government's gratitude. However, you must understand this is a military endeavor and as such, military-standard behavior is expected of everyone."

While Yorkson was wittering on, Taylan peered around the assembled heads. Where was Arthur? Kala Orr and her horrible son seemed to be absent too. Then she saw a face she recognized and gave a gasp of delight.

Abacha!

Wright nudged her.

"Now you're here," said Yorkson, "I can pass on more information that's recently come to our notice. As you're aware, the purpose of this mission is to address the threat a hostile alien species poses to human autonomy. These creatures have interfered in the course of human history, turning our political conflicts into games for their own sport. This cannot be tolerated, and so we must find them and challenge them. We must demand and insist they leave us alone, under the threat of an armed response if necessary. Admittedly, the *Defiant* is David compared to our enemy's Goliath, but we must do what we can with the resources we have to hand. You all know about the patterns identified in our new understanding of the universe that indicate we may be on the right path."

He inhaled deeply before saying, "We have also recently learned our mission is more urgent and important than ever. The skein mappers have identified signs the aliens have returned to Earth." Raising his voice over the murmurs of dismay and amazement his statement provoked, Yorkson continued, "The mappers haven't managed to narrow down the disturbance in the pattern to individuals yet. That may be something they're able to do during our absence. If they do, measures will be taken to eliminate the entities concerned."

Taylan's ears had pricked up. Finally, the admiral was saying something interesting. So Merlin and Morgan had come back? Or maybe different members of their species had decided to play their game. She recalled the visit to the Institute for Skein Studies and the complex web of connections joining the hundreds of people in the room. She couldn't imagine how complex a similar map of the globe might be or how the mappers might have discovered the new interference.

Then a realization hit. She turned to Wright. "You knew all about this, didn't you? That's what your secret conference with Colbourn was about."

He gave an apologetic smile.

"Wait," said Meilyr, rising to his feet. "No one gave us this information before we signed up. If we'd known, some of us might not have agreed to come along. Everyone here has left behind family and loved ones who might be in danger."

"Unfortunately, the information has only just come to light," Yorkson replied. "It arrived too late to alter any of the mission parameters, personnel included." The admiral stared at Meilyr in silence until the West BI native sat down.

The former Resistance leader looked seriously pissed off, and his brothers would follow his lead.

There could be trouble ahead.

12

—————

"They lied," Taylan muttered, digging into the BA's version of scrambled eggs. "The Alliance has known the aliens are back for months. They bloody lied, and I'm damned if I'm keeping my mouth shut about it."

Wright sighed and pinched the top of his nose between forefinger and thumb. "Please don't say anything. We're here now. There's no going back. Anything you tell your friends from West BI will only cause problems."

"They're not my friends. Most of them hate me, except Marc. But they're brave and loyal men, and they *don't* deserve to be lied to!" She threw down her fork in disgust. It bounced and landed on the deck with a clatter.

The noise drew attention in the refectory. When Taylan didn't move to pick it up, Wright stooped and scooped up the cutlery, placing it on the table as if the whole thing was an accident, not a display of Taylan's temper.

The diners returned to eating while Wright's new wife quietly seethed. She'd been uncommunicative since the meeting yesterday. He didn't think he'd ever seen her this angry, except maybe the night she'd kicked him out.

She narrowed her eyes at him. "You lied too."

"No, I didn't," he replied patiently. "I couldn't tell you what I knew. You aren't a Royal Marine anymore and even if you were your rank wouldn't have given you clearance."

"So you lied by omission. It's still a lie."

"What did you expect me to do? This is my job. I have rules I have to follow." Almost before the words were out of his mouth, he realized he'd said completely the wrong thing.

"So you put your job before our relationship? Before me?" Her expression had changed, her anger replaced by hurt. "You knew something that could influence my decision about joining the mission, and you chose not to tell me. Your work is more important to you than openness and honesty with your spouse."

Strictly speaking, she hadn't been his spouse at the time, but a belated sense of judgment told him this wasn't the moment to make the point. "I'm sorry, but my hands were tied. And I thought, in the circumstances, the best thing for you, Patrin, and Kayla would be to come on the mission. The signs in the skein indicated it was the right course of action. Who knows what'll go down on Earth now the aliens are back? You and your children could have been targeted."

"That's why you wanted us to get married? So I would come with you?" Tears glimmered in her eyes.

Wright silently cursed. Taylan was a strong woman, probably the strongest he'd ever met, in all senses of the word, yet he seemed to regularly reduce her to an emotional wreck. He reached over the table and covered her hand with his. "I love you, with all my heart and forever. *That's* why I wanted us to get married."

She didn't look convinced. Pushing her plate away, she stood up and walked off.

"Hey, Taylan," said a voice at Wright's side.

She must have heard but she didn't turn around.

"Abacha," said Wright. "Great to see you. Take a seat."

"What's up with her?" asked the corporal.

"It's nothing personal. She's looking forward to catching up with you. She just has a lot on her mind."

Taylan suddenly reappeared and gave Abacha a hug.

"Everything okay, little chick?" he asked.

"Everything's just fine." Taylan threw Wright a dirty look before stalking away again.

"Always was a pain in the ass," Abacha said. "What's got her goat this time? I thought she'd be okay now she got her kids back."

"We have a difference in opinion."

"That's all?"

"About something important."

"Shame. I was going to congratulate you guys on getting married, but I guess not."

"Maybe save it for later. Planning on starting up another xiangqi tournament?"

Abacha grinned. "You read my mind."

"Count me in, though I expect I won't make it through the first round as usual."

"Don't put yourself down. I bet you'll make round two at least." He glanced around the refectory with a predatory look. "Plenty of newbies in here. You'll have an advantage."

"I'll need it." Wright looked down at his bagel, his appetite gone. Then he remembered something that brightened his mood. "While you're here, I have some good news. Do you miss our time on the *Resolute*?"

"I do. It was fun, right? Aside from nearly dying in the Australian bush, I mean."

Wright chuckled. "Yeah, aside from that. You know we're picking up a few more personnel on Mars? Well, two of them are Ford and Krol."

"You're kidding? That's great news."

"They're both part of this, too, somehow."

Abacha's face fell. "Krol got pretty good at xiangqi on that deployment."

"So you'll have a worthy opponent. Someone to really test your abilities."

"Hmm, yeah." He frowned. "I'll need to up my game, but you're right. It'll be good for me. I'll ask the purser if I can print some medals. I'd better have extra for the runners up. I only hope I'm not one of them. Krol will never let me live it down."

"If it gets her talking, who cares?"

"I care. *I* care, man. Whoops, sorry. I mean, sir."

Wright waved dismissively. "Don't worry about it. Just watch out if Colbourn's around."

"Do you know how long it'll take us to reach Mars? I'm wondering if I should announce the tournament now or wait for the main voyage."

"Only two days, and that's traveling at nowhere near top speed."

Abacha whistled. "Two days to Mars? Who woulda thought it, even a few years ago?"

BY THE TIME the *Defiant* settled into Mars orbit, Taylan had started speaking to Wright again but her attitude remained cool. He didn't know what to say or do to make things better between them. He couldn't change the facts. He wasn't allowed to reveal sensitive information to people who didn't have clearance to hear it, not even his wife. And he had known Earth was under imminent threat when he proposed. He *had* wanted to get Taylan and her kids away. He couldn't deny any of it.

Then he thought of something that might convince her about his true feelings.

He didn't see her all day until the official ceremony to

welcome the remaining mission members boarding from Mars. Only military personnel were required to attend. Civilian participation was optional, but Taylan was here anyway. She hadn't mentioned she'd been planning to come. He hoped she was only curious to see who was coming aboard, not using the opportunity to demand a sudden exit. He wouldn't put it past her. She'd never been the best at following orders.

But Patrin and Kayla weren't here and Taylan would never abandon them.

Yorkson was dressed in full regalia, looking pompous and self-satisfied. It seemed a necessary characteristic of officers of the highest rank. Or maybe rising in the ranks made you that way. The rest of the military complement of the *Defiant's* crew had lined up along one side of the passageway. The few civilians stood in a less-straight line opposite.

Mars Station was an Alliance outpost, hence the formality. Yorkson had even arranged for the newcomers to be piped aboard.

The whistle sounded as the first arrivals emerged from the airlock.

There was Lieutenant Ford—now Captain Ford. The Australian sun had aged him. Wright allowed himself a flicker of a smile as they saluted and made eye contact. And there was Krol, her dour features betraying no sign of recognition. Never mind. She'd never been the most expressive person in the world. Was she up to speed with the new model of starship engine? He didn't doubt it. She'd probably been practicing xiangqi in the intervening years too.

Another figure appeared and Wright's heart warmed.

Iolani Hale had been working on the terraforming of Earth's sister planet, but now, as he understood, she would be responsible for the *Defiant's* green habitat. Heck, the ship probably only *had* a habitat due to her report on the voyage of the *Dauntless*. Had other measures been taken to mitigate the psychological effects of a deep-space journey? The last thing they needed was a repeat of the events on that trip, when several people had died and Iolani had nearly joined them.

All the newcomers had arrived. The airlock hatch closed and the two lines of greeters began to dissolve. The assigned Marine took Ford and Krol to their quarters. Wright approached Iolani for a less formal hello, but Taylan reached her first. The two women began to chat and he hesitated.

"Major Wright," Iolani called out as she noticed him. "There you are. I knew you were here but I couldn't spot you. You guys all look the same in uniform."

"He's a Lieutenant-Colonel now," Taylan corrected.

"You got promoted? Congratulations!"

"And we got married."

Wright lifted his eyebrows. What was going on? Was Taylan claiming her territory?

"Whoa, that's amazing," said Iolani. "I'm so happy for you." She hugged Taylan and then Wright. "You make a great couple. Listen, can I catch up with you two later? It's been a long day and I'm bushed. I'd like to get to my cabin and settle in. Try to make the place home. It's going to be a long voyage."

"Of course," Taylan said. "Maybe we can meet up for dinner."

Iolani left, and they were alone in the passageway. The sociable mask Taylan had been wearing dropped and her glum look of the last couple of days returned.

Wright decided not to ask her why she'd made a point of telling Iolani they were married. Nothing good could come of it, and if she had guessed feelings might have developed between him and the scientist during the *Dauntless*'s voyage, that wasn't unreasonable. Iolani *had* seemed to begin to see him as more than a friend at one point.

"Taylan, going back to our conversation at breakfast the other day..."

"Yeah?" she replied noncommittally, not making eye contact.

"I thought of something you might want to think about."

"What?"

At least she was prepared to be persuaded.

He took her left hand and lifted it, his fingers holding the two rings she wore, an engagement and a wedding ring. "If you remember, I proposed to you the same day we went to the Institute and Colbourn told me the skein mappers had spotted the aliens' return. We went straight home afterward and then out for our walk, right? I didn't have time to go and buy a ring and I didn't need to because I'd bought it days before. I had it with me all the time. I didn't propose to you because of what I'd just learned."

Her shoulders rose and fell. "You're right. I remember."

"You believe me?"

She finally met his gaze. "I believe you."

"So things are okay now between us?"

"Yes."

"You don't seem very happy about it."

"Now I have to worry even more about losing you."

13

———

The cutting-edge tech upgrades and final checks for the *Defiant* would take around ten days. To help pass the time, Iolani had offered to take Taylan, Wright, Patrin, and Kayla on a Mars Station tour. She'd been working as a consultant on the terraforming of the planet since returning from the voyage of the *Dauntless*.

"It isn't going well," she said ruefully as the shuttle took them down to the surface. "Kekoa has done her best, but there's so much we still don't know."

She was referring to the sixth member of their party. Taylan hadn't noticed her in particular when she'd boarded the *Defiant* yesterday. Kekoa was apparently another mission member identified by the skein mappers for her place in the pattern.

"It's been one headache after another, right from the start," she echoed. Like Iolani, Kekoa was small, dark-haired, and olive-skinned. "The Alliance asked me to oversee the terraforming due to my work experience on the *Bres*, but creating ecosystems on a planet is a whole other ball game, as I soon found out."

"You used to work for Ua Talman?" asked Taylan.

"I was Director of Habitats on the Antarctic Project. It was how Iolani and I met. When Lorcan decided to strip all three ships down to bare bones and start again, I was out of a job. He offered to pay a retainer until he needed me again, but I would have been bored out of my head with nothing to do, so I jumped at the Alliance's offer. Took me about six months to realize I'd made a mistake. Since then, I think it's only my own sheer pigheadedness that's kept me going."

"You did a great job in the circumstances," said Iolani, squeezing Kekoa's hand.

They shared a look that told Taylan she hadn't needed to have any concerns about Iolani and Wright's friendship.

"Attempts to terraform Mars have been going on for more than a millennium," Iolani continued. "The work you did means we're closer now than ever."

"Maybe," Kekoa answered. "I'm looking forward to seeing how things progress while we're gone. It's kind of handy to have the opportunity to jump forward a few years. The processes are so slow and Mars is so big, it's like trying to watch evolution in action."

"How many years will we be gone, I wonder?" said Iolani.

That was the big question. For the journey of the *Dauntless*, it had been easy for astrophysicists to compute exactly how much time would pass on Earth while the ship traveled through interstellar space. The calculation for the *Defiant's* voyage was not so clear cut. It was why Taylan had never even contemplated leaving Patrin and Kayla behind and under-taking the mission without them. Aside from the fact they were too young to be left without a parent, there was no way she was going to miss out on years of their lives—perhaps all the life they had.

"You were both so lucky working for Uncle Lorcan," Kayla said. "He's lovely."

Iolani, who had been taking a sip of coffee, spat out her drink all over herself and commenced a fit of coughing. Kekoa patted her back while also dabbing at her clothes with napkins while quietly chuckling for some reason.

"Sorry," Iolani croaked. "Went down the wrong way."

"Mam," said Kayla, "will we see Arthur while we're down there?"

Taylan suspected she'd grown a little jealous of the attention Patrin had received from the king on their horse-riding excursions. "I don't think so, sweetheart. He's on an official visit. All his time will be taken up with meetings and social events."

"You should have plenty more opportunities to see him after we set off," Wright said. "He'll have lots of free time. Everyone's schedule will become much less hectic."

"Yes," said Iolani, turning in her seat to face Kayla. "It'll be hard to find stuff to do to keep ourselves occupied. You'll have lots of chances to spend time with Arthur."

Kekoa laughed and shook her head. "Listen to you guys! On first-name terms with the King of the Britannic Isles."

Taylan said, "So will you be before long. He's very approachable."

"That's the impression I have," Kekoa replied, "which is why it makes even less sense he's married to that she-devil Dwyr Orr. It's a marriage of convenience, right? Has to be."

"You didn't hear it from me," Wright joked.

"Is the Dwyr taking part in the ceremonies?" asked Patrin.

Wright snorted his disgust. "Yeah, she'll be there. She won't miss out on an opportunity to show off. Her slimy son is with her too."

~

Exiting the shuttle, Taylan hoped her and Arthur's paths might cross on Mars, even though it was unlikely. She hadn't seen him aboard the *Defiant* yet. She wasn't sure why, but he, Orr, and Orr's son hadn't mingled with the rest of the passengers at all, as far as she knew. The Alliance couldn't keep the BI's royalty separate from everyone else forever, at least not the king. Orr and Little-Orr could spend the entire voyage in the brig as far as she was concerned.

Beyond the shuttle landing pad, red Martian dust covered the ground between concrete pathways and more landing pads. The dust lay in a fine layer on everything else and tinged the sky pink-orange.

She hadn't seen Arthur much at all since his return to Earth, and she missed him. It was odd. There had been a time she'd feared him and been appalled by his behavior, but now she didn't think it was his true nature—more what he felt compelled to do. Realizing everything he'd done was due to Merlin and Morgan's manipulations must have been devastating.

EVA suits were still required for getting about on Mars. A spaceport official made the party wait at the base of the ramp while he checked their suits' stats. Taylan brought up the environment levels on her visor overlay. Oxygen sat at 5.5 percent. CO_2 still comprised most of the planet's atmosphere. Terraforming definitely wasn't going well.

"Okay," said the official via comm, "you're all fine and cleared to go. Follow the red arrows to Immigration."

"I feel so much lighter!" Kayla exclaimed. "This is cool." She jumped, rising far off the ground before descending.

Taylan said, "Can you save the acrobatics until we're outside the spaceport?"

"I'm surprised this isn't all enclosed," Wright remarked as they walked along.

"Most Martian bases *are* enclosed," said Kekoa. "Almost everything is underground. Only the spaceports are above ground, for the shuttle landings."

"Bases?" Kayla asked. "Don't you mean towns?"

"Er, no. There are no towns here. Just research bases and mine sites. Though I suppose you could call the miners' residences towns of a kind. They've expanded a lot since Lorcan shifted all his operations off Earth."

"But I thought we were colonizing Mars," said Kayla.

"What would be the point of that?" asked Patrin. "Even the most inhospitable places on Earth are way easier for humans to survive in than anywhere on Mars."

"Your brother's right," said Iolani. "People used to talk about Mars colonization programs hundreds of years ago but no one's thought it's a good idea for a long time. There are too many disadvantages to make it worthwhile."

"Like what?" Kayla took a leap and sailed upward. "I'd love it."

"You wouldn't like the effects of low gravity on your bones," said Kekoa. "To avoid long-term damage I had to spend at least half my days here in a chamber that created Earth-equivalent gravity. And then there's the radiation. Unless we somehow manage to kick-start a magnetosphere, it isn't going away anytime soon. Martians will have to live underground or in radiation-proof habitations, rarely going outside. And when they do go outside, in most places it's too cold to take off EVA suits. Would you like that?"

"Hm. Maybe not."

"Just some of the problems we face with terraforming," Kekoa said to the group generally. "Very few organisms survive here, only a handful of species that metabolize CO_2 and hydrogen. The radiation, cold, or low atmospheric pressure kills most everything else eventually."

After passing the immigration checks, Kekoa requested a transport to take them to Valles Marineris Minor. As the vehicle took them down into a tunnel, Kekoa explained that the underground road and rail network covered most of the vast valley. "It was built in more optimistic times. The minimal activity in the crust has kept it stable all these years."

Lights flashed past as the vehicle sped along.

Patrin asked, "Do the tunnels have atmosphere?"

"No," replied Kekoa. "They're way too leaky. You can only take off your suit inside a base, and then you must always check the readings on your visor beforehand. Even so, there have been accidents. Everyone here always sleeps with a suit under their bed, just in case."

"It sounds worse and worse!" Kayla exclaimed.

"Are you happy you aren't staying now?" asked Wright.

She folded her arms and didn't answer.

They didn't stay long at Kekoa's now former home. The labs and living quarters were the same as you might expect to see on Earth, only perhaps barer and smellier. The place had a forgotten air about it. Taylan was reminded of the preserved bases of the old explorers on Earth, their diaries, equipment, and rations frozen in time.

Soon, they were above ground again, Kekoa driving them in a transparent-roofed buggy over the rocky Martian landscape. "It's a little bit rougher than the underground network," she apologized. "There are well-worn tracks but no paved roads on the surface."

"You know, things might improve quickly here while we're gone," Taylan commented. "It looks like the new tech hasn't hit Mars yet. Once it does, it'll be a game-changer."

"Maybe," replied Kekoa. "No doubt the little red planet will be an afterthought as usual."

Looking at the surroundings, it was hard to imagine much terraforming had gone on here. The place seemed about as barren as it could get. Lifeless desert stretched to the horizon on every side. The Australian outback was abundant in comparison.

But then Taylan spotted shapes that diverged from the norm up ahead. "What's that?"

"Ah," Kekoa replied, smiling, "you've spotted my pride and joy."

As they neared the rounded outlines standing out against the pink sky, their color intensified. On Earth, it would have looked pale and wan, here the soft green seemed remarkable, almost alien.

The results of Kekoa's years of work stood about three meters high at their tallest. Clumps of smaller examples of the —plant? fungus?—had sprouted around the largest specimens.

They climbed out of the buggy and approached the life growing miraculously in a highly inhospitable environment. Forty or fifty specimens dotted the ground in an area spanning twenty or so meters.

Touching the tallest one proudly, Kekoa said, "I realized trying to get Earth species to grow on Mars was just about pointless. They all evolved to survive on another planet, and while succeeding generations would adapt to the conditions, natural selection has been slow so far. Even the first species we seeded Mars with centuries ago are still only clinging on. So I decided to go a different route and genetically engineered completely new organisms from the basics up. Living here meant I could test them on a daily basis, tweaking and improving as I went along."

"You did a fantastic job," said Iolani. "They're amazing."

Amazing was a strong word for the non-descript lumps poking up from the dry, frozen Martian soil. Taylan struggled for something genuinely positive to say.

"That's *it*?" Kayla whispered.

Unfortunately, because she was speaking via comm, everyone heard her.

Patrin said, "Kayla, how many times have you been told to watch what you s—."

A brilliant flash lit up the sky from horizon to horizon and a dull rumble resounded underfoot.

14

———

Shock silenced the little group, and then Kayla said, "I'm guessing that wasn't supposed to happen."

"No," said Kekoa. "We sometimes feel detonations from mining operations, but nothing like that. Something's gone very wrong. I hope no one's hurt."

"Wright?" came Colbourn's comm.

"Yes, ma'am?"

"Get over to Valles Marineris Major immediately. There's been an attack on Arthur and Orr."

"Wilco. Where are they exactly?"

"Just get moving. I'll send precise coordinates as soon as I have them." She cut the comm.

The brigadier knew he was on the surface but she didn't know who he was with. None of the others carried military implants.

He hesitated. "I have orders to drive to Valles Marineris Major. Can you all return by yourselves to—"

"Not a chance," said Kekoa. "It's a three-hour walk. We'd be pushing our suits' O2 supplies."

"What's going on?" asked Taylan

"Then you'll all have to come with me. I'll explain on the way."

They bundled into the buggy.

Colbourn drip fed Wright details on the attack as he guided the vehicle over the rocky ground. The royal pair had been visiting the main research base when as-yet unidentified assailants had ambushed them and their entourage in a particularly inaccessible section. The commander of the base's small military contingent had been killed in the initial assault, and his second-in-command had only just arrived on Mars.

Wright considered the fact that *he'd* only been on Mars less than a couple of hours, but clearly Colbourn wanted him to take control of the situation, probably due to his history with Arthur and Orr.

"But why would anyone want to assassinate Arthur and the Dwyr?" Kayla asked. "It doesn't make any sense."

"People do all kinds of crazy things for crazy reasons," Iolani replied, "and sometimes for no reason at all. Humans are dumb like that."

Her comment gave Wright an idea about what might be happening at VM Major, but he kept it to himself.

"Kids," Taylan said, "when we get there I want both of you to stay in this vehicle with Iolani and Kekoa."

"Aren't you staying with us?" asked Kayla.

"I'm going to help Wright."

"No," he objected. "Taylan, you—"

"You'll need everyone you can get, and I know what I'm doing."

He couldn't deny the truth of her words.

"I want to come too," said Patrin. "I want to help Arthur."

Taylan said, "That's brave of you, son, but I can't allow it. It's too dangerous."

"Your mother's right," said Iolani. "Stay here with us."

"But I've done my training," Patrin protested.

"Training and fighting are two different things," Taylan said. "This isn't a discussion. I'm telling you you're staying here."

He frowned angrily but didn't argue.

The cause of the flash in the sky became apparent a kilometer from their destination. A gigantic hole had been blown open in the landscape. Debris had been scattered far and wide and a thick, pale red haze hung in the thin Martian air.

"Shit," Wright muttered, maneuvering the buggy around the shattered remains of a large boulder.

Kekoa sucked in a shocked breath. "The section will have lost atmosphere."

"What happens in a depressurization event?" Wright asked.

"After a ten-second warning, the doors nearest the breach will seal. If you don't make it through them in time, you have to put on an EVA suit and reach a pressurized area from the outside."

"So there are suits stored in every section?"

"Usually, there would be at least one for every person who regularly works in the area, but if a large group was moving through when the explosion occurred..."

She didn't need to go on. Whoever planned the attack would have made sure they had suits to survive the aftereffects, but those under attack were not so lucky. There could be people dead of asphyxiation already.

"Look out!" yelled Taylan.

Wright avoided the obstacle just in time.

"What was it?" Kayla asked, rising from her seat and craning to look.

"Sit down," Taylan ordered, "and face forward."

The object Wright had nearly driven over was the corpse of a young woman, a scientist, judging from her lab coat, her body broken. She must have been at the epicenter of the blast. Wright had only caught a glimpse of her before hearing Taylan's warning, but the snapshot image burned in his mind.

He gripped the steering wheel, his knuckles turning white as he fought off the specter of Patel's ruined face threatening from the corners of his vision.

"Where's the nearest tunnel entrance to this section?" he asked Kekoa, frustrated that Colbourn hadn't yet relayed the information.

"Uh, about a klick that way," she replied, pointing northeast.

That was why the brigadier had only given him the detonation coordinates. Trying to reach the area via underground roads would take too much time. He would have to go in through the hole. He asked Colbourn to patch him into the comm network of the Marines on site. It had already been thirteen minutes since the explosion

"Lieutenant Lethen? SITREP."

"Still trying to locate King Arthur, Dwyr Orr, and her son, sir. Needless to say, they aren't answering comms. We have many dead and injured. I have fifteen operational personnel, ten more en route. I've assigned fireteams to find survivors and move them to a safe location while the rest of us go after the king and the dwyr."

"Any word from the attackers?"

"Nothing, sir."

"Do you know who they are?" he asked as he and Taylan exited the buggy.

"Not a clue. I don't know who would do such a thing. The bomb blew out a huge area just after the inspection party passed through. It's...it's carnage down here." Her voice wobbled as she came to the end of her sentence.

"All right, Lieutenant. Keep it together. I'll be there in two minutes. I'll need your guidance on where to get in."

"That won't be hard, sir. The place is open to the sky nearly everywhere."

She wasn't exaggerating. As he approached the hole in the

ground, a huge area of the underground complex became visible. The bomb had collapsed walls at the epicenter. Farther away, furniture had been blasted apart and burned. Though the bodies of those who hadn't reached an EVA suit in time could be seen here and there, at least the loss of atmosphere had dampened fires. Otherwise, the entire place could have been incinerated.

"We'd better climb in over there," said Taylan, "where the ground looks most stable."

He made visual contact with Lieutenant Lethen. She waved back, and when he indicated where he would try to gain access to the site, she comm'd, "That's as good a place as any, sir. I'll meet you there."

A crumbling cliff face of Martian subsoil and rock, broken concrete, and twisted rebar confronted them at the spot Taylan had proposed. His civilian visor overlay didn't display distances as a HUD would but he estimated the drop to be twelve meters. They could try to climb down the treacherous surface, risking it collapsing and trapping them under the rubble, or they could jump.

"What do you think?" Taylan asked.

"We're at less than half gravity. I'll aim for that bit of clear ground. If I break something, you try a different way."

"No, you're more important than me."

Before he could stop her, she leapt into the chasm.

The slower passage of her body moving in point-four G looked odd. She landed and rolled, the breathy noise of her impact sounding over her comm. Standing, she briefly shook her legs and arms and then gave him a thumbs-up. In another couple of seconds he was beside her, inside the demolished remains of the section of VM Major.

"Boy, am I glad to see you two," said Lethen, jogging toward them.

"Remember where you are, Lieutenant," Wright barked. He

couldn't afford to have her drop the ball now a superior officer had arrived.

"Yes, sir. Sorry, sir."

"You seem to have the situation under control here. Where were Arthur and Orr last seen before the bomb went off?"

"I'll take you there. The area is choked with debris. We're trying to clear it but it's slow work. We don't have machinery to do the heavy lifting."

"I imagine that was the hostiles' intention," said Wright. "They waited until their targets were out of serious danger before setting off the bomb, anticipating the damage would hamper pursuit."

"Taylan?"

It was Kekoa. His comm remained open to the civilian channel he'd been using with her and the others.

"Yes?" Taylan responded. "What is it?"

"I'm really sorry, but Patrin and Kayla got away."

"*What*?"

"They've left the vehicle. They must have some kind of secret signal system. They jumped out together and ran off. There was nothing Iolani or I could do to stop them. I think they plan on helping you guys."

Wright thought the same, though the idiot children only added to his problems. "Taylan, tell them—"

"I know. I'm on it." She sounded as irritated as he felt.

"Lead the way, Lieutenant."

15

———

Marines moved slowly among the rubble at the caved-in entrance to a passageway, carrying lumps of concrete and levering others from the piles. They were at a far side of the destroyed section, under a jagged-edged roof. Deep cracks ran at all angles across the ceiling, forewarning of imminent collapse.

"What a nightmare," said Wright on a one-to-one channel with Taylan.

She'd kept him out of her comms with her kids. He could just imagine the lashing they were receiving.

"You two," he said, addressing a pair of Marines pulling a body out from a recently excavated mound. "Leave that. Look for beams, posts, anything you can find to prop up this ceiling. Lethen, get all your people working in here. I want access to that tunnel and I need two pulse rifles, beamers, and knives."

"Yes, sir."

"What's happening in the section ahead? How much of the area has depressurized?"

"Don't know, sir. The main system hasn't received any readings from the sensors there since the blast. In theory, a door about fifty meters down the passageway should have sealed."

"Should there be people beyond it?"

"Yes, but not many. It's a storage section. A warehouse. A road runs to it direct from the spaceport."

As soon as a narrow space at the top of the blocked tunnel was cleared, Taylan climbed up to it and peered in, the blackness beyond dissolving as her helmet light activated. "Looks pretty empty on this side."

Whoever had placed the bomb had done an excellent job. This was not the work of amateurs or opportunists. The attack had been carefully planned and carried out.

Without another word, Taylan disappeared into the gap.

Dammit.

He scrambled up after her, telling Lethen to continue clearing the space then to send in a team to rendezvous with him on the other side.

"Taylan, hold on," he said as he reached the narrow void.

"Patrin and Kayla are in here. They've turned off their comms, but Kekoa just told me she spotted them running into the tunnel entrance."

"Huh?" He dropped the weapons Lethen had given him through the hole and then eased himself into it feet first. "She said that was a kilometer away."

"And this is Martian gravity."

Great.

Now they had to rescue two errant children as well as Arthur, Orr, and her son.

His body dangled, his shoulders caught on the jagged opening. After some twisting and turning as the rocky surface grated against his suit, he dropped to the ground and picked up the weapons. Taylan had jogged ahead while he'd been making his way in. He asked her to wait and, for once, she complied.

"Our visors have night vision," he said when he caught up

to her. He handed her a rifle, beamer, and knife. "Turn off your helmet light."

The bright beam would be a clear signal to the kidnappers.

"Where am I supposed to put these?" she asked. She'd slung the rifle over her shoulder but their EVA suits had nowhere to stow the other weapons.

"Just hold them."

He muttered a curse. They were not well-prepared for facing armed hostiles. Their suits weren't even armored.

They set off.

In the time it had taken them to reach the explosion site plus the additional minutes spent arriving in the passageway, the attackers could have moved far. Perhaps they could even have reached an escape vehicle. But they would have been seen leaving.

After passing one empty room—some kind of office—they hit closed double doors across the passage. This had to be the warehouse entrance Lethen had mentioned. As she'd predicted, the doors were sealed.

"Lethen?" Wright comm'd.

"Yes, sir."

"Is there a security override code for this area?" He prayed he didn't need an official's bio signatures.

"Yes, sir, but you can't input it. I know where you are. I can open that seal remotely but the section beyond it will depressurize."

"Do it." He turned to Taylan. "We have to move back."

There was no shelter. Before they'd gone a few meters, the doors whipped open, air flooded out and debris began to fly down the passage. Mars wasn't a vacuum, but its atmosphere remained much thinner than Earth's. The evening up of the pressure difference moved surprisingly large items. A desk dragged past, a chair caught underneath it.

"Uh, sir," said Lethen, "we've opened up the gap you went

through and I'm sending Marines through to back you up, but all this stuff flying down here is going to hamper them."

"It can't be helped. Do what you can."

"Won't Arthur die if we don't reach him quickly now?" Taylan asked. "What if the attackers don't give him a suit?"

"I'm not sure what'll happen. I saw him survive a complete vacuum once." That had been on the *Dauntless* when the Merlins and Morgans had attacked. He wasn't sure if the protection the king had enjoyed then still applied. Taylan hadn't mentioned Orr, but the Dwyr had seemed sure she would also survive deep space. Whether her son possessed the same ability was another question.

Nevertheless, they couldn't waste any more time. "Let's go."

Pushing against the escaping air and avoiding the occasional flying object, they returned down the passageway. No lights lit the warehouse interior, not even emergency lighting. Someone had darkened the place. His night vision revealed wide shelves rising on each side to the high ceiling, their contents slowly sliding off.

"Watch out!" He pushed Taylan out of the way just in time as a box plummeted to the ground and split, scattering metal parts.

"We should stay in the center of the aisles," he said.

"We need cover."

She was right. It was a toss up between being hit by falling packaged goods or being shot at. They moved to the edge and continued walking slowly forward, casting frequent upward glances. The escape of the atmosphere appeared to be slowing down.

"At least Patrin and Kayla can't be in here," said Taylan. "They wouldn't have been able to get in."

"Sir," said Lethen via comm, "I've just received notification the outer airlock was opened from the inside."

What the hell?

He gave Taylan the bad news and winced at the barrage of foul language she issued.

"How on Earth did they get in?" she finally asked.

"It might not be the kids," he replied. "It could be the attackers leaving."

It was not the attackers leaving. At least, not the ones who had kidnapped the royal party.

"I demand to be returned to my rightful position!"

Orr had stepped in front of them. Though she wore an EVA suit, her bearing made her unmistakable. The also-suited figure flanking her on her right seemed to be her son. Another man stood assertively to her left.

Wright halted. "Where's Arthur?" he asked via external comm, casting the weapons in his hands aside and lifting his rifle to his shoulder.

He expected Taylan to do the same, but she'd vanished.

"He's choking out the remainder of his life not far from here," Orr replied. "If the Alliance wants him to live, they must return me and my son to Earth and restore all our rights. I will hold Arthur hostage until my demands are met."

"He doesn't need to breathe air."

"That was my guess too, but I was wrong and so are you."

"Then you need to give him a suit or you'll kill your only bargaining chip."

"Don't worry, my loyal Crusaders are seeing to it. Finding one to fit him proved somewhat of a challenge."

The tightness in Wright's chest eased. Arthur wasn't about to die. "You're insane, Orr, if you think you'll get off an Alliance outpost alive. Our military has this place surrounded."

"Your confidence is misguided, Wright. My people have infiltrated every sector of Mars Station. I have miners, technicians, cleaners, even scientists here. You never know, perhaps some of your military are also secretly devoted to me. And you dare not kill me. Not yet. Not while we're so close to Earth. The BA still needs the compliance of Crusaders."

He wasn't so sure she was correct. The Alliance was allowing her to live because of her significance in the skein. A few fundamentalist fanatics remained, but, politically, the EAC was dead.

"My communication will have reached the BI Government by now," said Orr. "Neither I nor it has any further need of you." Her head turned to the man at her side as if she was issuing him a command.

Before he could follow it, Wright ducked behind some shelving, slung his rifle over his back, and ran. Where was Taylan? He didn't want to risk comming her. Without encryption, Orr's followers at the station might be able to tap into their conversation.

The metal units on each side of him whipped past. He reached the end of the row and checked from side to side. Nothing but shelves and the scattered contents they had once held.

A burst of light and a fierce *hiss* erupted next to his head. He was being fired on.

He darted into the space and ran several rows down before darting into one.

Taylan had to be searching for Arthur, or perhaps her kids. Where were they and how had they managed to get in? Orr hadn't mentioned a word about them.

Stores packed the shelves here, clearly items too heavy to be dragged off when the place depressurized. He arrived at a wall, hoping for an opening but meeting a dead end. He would have to go back.

Or would he?

His gaze traveled up the shelving. It seemed to stop before it reached the ceiling, leaving a gap. He had no time to figure out for sure. He climbed onto the lowest tier and stretched to reach the one above. His fingertips grasped the edge. He hauled himself up, putting over an elbow and then a knee. Running footsteps sounded nearby, faint in the thin air.

Quickly sliding into a recess between two boxes, he held his breath and waited.

The footsteps stopped.

A beat passed, and then they started up again.

Wright climbed the rest of the way to the top.

A steel and cardboard landscape spread out all around, the ceiling roughly a couple of meters above.

He spotted movement.

Like a bird on a perch, a figure squatted on a shelf some distance away, waving.

Taylan.

She pointed downward.

She'd found Arthur.

16

———

Thin struts linked each set of shelving. There was no other way of traveling between them without descending to the floor. Taylan had been smart to take this other route around the warehouse—it would be a while before Orr's goons thought to look above their heads—but she was better suited than him for balancing on the connecting strips. If he fell, he probably wouldn't break anything due to the low gravity, but the noise would give him away immediately and, as Orr had pointed out, she had no reason to spare his life.

He crawled to the aisle end of the shelving, where a strut branched out to the next set. From his high vantage point, more of Orr's Crusaders were visible, walking along the aisles, searching for him. Two women who had presumably been faithful to Alliance sprawled out, lifeless, their torsos marked with pulse rounds.

The strut was about as wide as his palm. He could try to walk it like a tightrope, but... No. He couldn't stand upright. The ceiling was too low. He would be forced to bend over, and four limbs were more stable than two anyway. He slid one hand down the strut, reaching out, before following it with his other hand. His right knee came next. Then... How to do this?

Taylan was gesturing at him frantically. Something was happening and she needed his help.

He brought his left knee forward, but there was nowhere for it to go. He wobbled. He tried to move back, but his right knee slipped off the strut. As he fell, he managed to grab it with his hands. For a second he hung like a monkey in a tree.

"There he is!"

As he heaved himself up a pulse round hissed past. He leapt onto the strut and ran along it, stooping.

Pain exploded from his thighs.

He'd been hit.

Taylan was up and racing toward him, raining pulses down on his attackers.

He made it to the next set of shelves but then collapsed. The sensation from his legs was agonizing. He couldn't move and his suit was losing air.

Taylan was at his side. "Get me an EVA suit!" she yelled, her voice echoing despite thin atmosphere. "Orr, get me a fucking suit. If he dies I'll come down there and kill you. You know I can do it."

His chest labored as his lungs fought for oxygen.

He was fading. The ceiling seemed to move away, and then it turned black.

HE CAME to with the feeling he'd been roughly manhandled. But he could breathe again. He inhaled deeply and opened his eyes. He was looking at the same ceiling he'd seen as he passed out. His thighs felt like they were on fire.

There was Taylan.

"I didn't die," he said.

She tilted her head, puzzled.

He switched to external comm and softly repeated himself.

"No, you made it," she replied, "though you're damned hard to get out of and into a suit. Orr values her life very highly." Leaning out a little, she went on, louder, "Isn't that right, my dear Dwyr? Not going to take even the slightest chance I might get you."

A pulse round flew past and scorched the concrete above.

Kala Orr's voice drifted up. "Enjoy your brief remaining moments, Taylan Ellis. You're trapped. I hold all the cards. Your weapon will run out of power eventually and my soldiers will overwhelm you. Then you won't be a danger to me any longer."

Taylan leaned close and whispered, "She thinks only Arthur and I can kill her."

"She does? Another Crusader delusion."

Taylan shrugged. "Lucky for you anyway."

The Dwyr's comments on the *Dauntless* began to make sense. She'd said something about drifting in space, unable to die, if he put her out the airlock.

Whatever the woman was on, it was strong stuff.

"Orr's got a point," Taylan said. "We *are* trapped."

"What's happened to Lethen? She should be here by now."

"There was some fighting over by the door while you were out. I think we caught a break getting in when we did. The Crusaders were still recovering from the depressurization."

"I only spotted a handful of them," Wright said. "How about you?"

"The same. Arthur's over there." She nodded toward the corner he'd seen her at before.

"I thought so."

"He only has three Crusaders guarding him but I couldn't get a clear shot at all of them. I was hoping you could take out one or two from another direction."

"I don't think I'm in a fit state to take out anyone right

now." The pain from his wounded thighs was rapidly intensifying as his adrenaline faded. If only he were armored up. He would have the benefit of rapid-effect analgesics. Doing it the old-fashioned way sucked. "I don't even think I can move. Sorry."

"Don't apologize for staying alive, nitwit."

"If I hadn't persuaded you to join the mission, I'd be d—"

"I knew you had an ulterior motive. Shut up, okay? Don't waste your energy. I need to figure this out."

But what could she possibly figure out? They were surrounded by Crusaders and an untold number also occupied roles all over the station. Orr's plan to force the Alliance to return her to Earth under threat of killing Arthur could easily succeed. The BA wanted and needed their king, if not to maintain political control on Earth then to play his part in preventing the aliens' interference. They might give up a lot to keep him alive, including a certain lieutenant-colonel and maybe even Taylan.

The surface he was lying on shook in a tell-tale manner. Taylan clearly felt it too. She reached out with her rifle, pointed the muzzle downward, and fired. The shelving shuddered and a thud resounded from below.

"The higher ground always carries the advantage," she muttered. "That's what Dad always said." After a pause, she added, "Dammit, Wright! What are we going to do?"

She appeared to be reaching the same conclusion he had a moment earlier: they were screwed.

Then a shriek rent the air. "GONE! What do you mean, he's gone?!"

Taylan peeked over the edge of the shelf. "The Dwyr's losing her shit. I think she doesn't have Arthur anymore. He must have got away somehow. I'm gonna..."

She wanted to take advantage of Orr's distraction.

"Go," he said. "I'll be fine." He pulled himself painfully onto his elbows and lifted the rifle Taylan had placed by his side. "I will. I have this. Go and do your stuff."

"I wish I could kiss you." She bumped her visor against his and disappeared.

Pulses hissed, momentarily whiting out his night vision with their flashes. There were shouts and the running of booted feet. An agonized scream rang out. Vague, meaningless sounds reached him.

Then a hush fell.

Wright strained his hearing. What was going on? Had the voice screaming been Taylan's?

He tried to pull himself closer to the edge of the shelf to see what was happening, but the slightest movement of his legs brought paralyzing pain. He lay down again, cursing his feebleness and impotence. What if Orr had caught Taylan? What if she had killed her while he was lying here, useless?

His resting place juddered. Someone was climbing up. If it was Taylan, she would call out and warn him.

No sound came from the climber.

He angled his rifle to point at the place he guessed the person would emerge. He would get only one chance to take them out, and only then if they were stupid enough to expose themselves before firing. Staring at the spot where he antici-pated his attacker would appear, he rested his finger lightly on the trigger.

A head rose up.

It wasn't Taylan's.

He fired.

At the last second he realized his mistake and managed to jerk the rifle a fraction. The shot kissed the figure's helmet before it went wide.

The head ducked down.

"It's Kayla! Please don't shoot."

"Stars, Kayla! I could have killed you. Are you okay?"

She reappeared and nodded. "It's my fault. Mam told me to warn you I was coming up, but I forgot. I wanted to see you were all right. She said you got shot. Are you okay?"

"I'm all the better for not murdering you."

As they'd been talking, the shelves had begun moving again. Someone else was climbing up.

Another head appeared opposite Kayla's.

Patrin.

"Thank the stars you're still alive, TJ," he said. "Hold on just another minute. Arthur's coming to help get you down."

"Arthur?" Wright asked. "He's free?"

"Patrin and I did it," said Kayla excitedly. "It was so cool. They didn't suspect us right until the end, did they, Patrin?"

"No, they didn't. Dumb Crusaders."

"What did you do?"

"I'll tell you later," Patrin replied. "I'd better help you down quick or Mam'll kill me."

17

The atmosphere in the cabin on the shuttle journey back to the *Defiant* was far different than it had been on the ride down to the surface of Mars. Kekoa and Iolani sat silently holding hands, and Taylan was quiet and pensive. Wright was still in pain despite the analgesics the Martian doctor had dispensed. She'd said he needed to remain conscious for his medical assessment when he arrived back on the ship. Only Patrin and Kayla were bright and upbeat, swapping remarks on the events in the Crusader attack. Even Arthur, usually mild-tempered whenever he wasn't in battle, seemed morose and lost in thought. He was joining them for immediate evacuation to the ship, while Orr and her son would stay on Mars until the station director determined who among his staff was secretly a Crusader.

Wright reckoned he knew what Arthur was thinking about.

In the skirmish, while Taylan's children had done whatever it was they did to free him—they hadn't explained yet—he'd been hit by pulse fire. Like Wright, he'd been wearing a civilian EVA suit, which was utterly useless to protect against an armed attack. Arthur had been hit in the midriff, and the doc would have only given him sufficient meds to take the edge off the pain. From the expression on his face as he lay across the seating, he was suffering just as much as Wright. But that probably wasn't the main cause of his worries.

Arthur should not have been vulnerable to pulse rounds at all. In every fight ever since he'd been brought back to life the energy bolts had slid over him, harmless as a puff of wind. Today's battle had been the first time he'd actually been hit. And Orr had said she'd needed to find him an EVA suit when the warehouse depressurized. When the *Dauntless* had been attacked, Arthur had survived the vacuum of space.

He wasn't only aging, he was becoming more human in other ways too.

He was becoming mortal.

"Hey kids," Wright called out.

"Yes, TJ?" Patrin replied.

"Come here and tell me what you did in the warehouse. I still don't understand how you managed to get in." Perhaps Arthur would be glad of the distraction too.

Taylan, sitting in the aisle seat in front of the king, looked up sadly. "Please don't encourage them, Wright." She had to be ruing her decision to allow her children to join the mission. Patrin and Kayla were high on the excitement and triumph of their plan's success, but things could easily have gone differently.

The pair ignored their mother and climbed into the seats in front of him, leaning over their backs to talk.

"As soon as I saw the explosion," said Patrin, "I figured out it had to be Crusaders. They love that shit."

"Patrin," Taylan said, a stern note in her voice, "don't swear."

Wright blinked and looked at her, wide-eyed.

She stared back. "What?"

His volume a notch lower, the boy continued, "I knew Kekoa and Iolani would never allow us to leave the vehicle, but

I also knew we could help you guys and Arthur a lot. None of you know Crusaders like I do."

Taylan silently shook her head.

"Me too!" Kayla protested.

"Yeah," Patrin conceded reluctantly. "Honestly, sis, it was more like you would never have let me go alone."

Kayla grinned. "That's true."

"Do you two have a secret sign language?" asked Wright, remembering Kekoa's remark.

"Yes," the woman in question echoed, apparently overhearing. She leaned out into the aisle, looking back. "Do you?"

"Not really," said Patrin. "But we've grown up together. We get each other, right, Kayla?"

"Yeah. I could tell from his face what he was planning." She added to Kekoa, "Sorry about running off like that."

Kekoa replied, "I guess it all came out in the wash in the end."

"I thought," said Patrin, "if I talked to them in the right accent, telling them we were here to help, they would let us in. And they did."

"Couldn't they tell you were just kids?" Wright asked, then immediately regretted the question as he registered Patrin's offended look. "I mean, adolescents." He wasn't sure if his correction made a difference.

"Do we look like kids in our EVA suits?" asked Kayla.

"Good point." The suits' tinted visors would have prevented the Crusaders from seeing their faces clearly, and Patrin was taller and bulkier even than him. Kayla was a fair height, too, for a thirteen-year-old girl.

"After the place depressurized," Patrin went on, "I think they were keen to have some more hands on deck."

"It was incredibly risky!" Taylan exclaimed. "How could you have been so sure Kala Orr had other operatives at the station? They could have guessed what you were up to and killed you."

"I'm sorry, Mam," Patrin replied, "but there was no way the EAC would be able to arrange a blast like that without the place being riddled with Crusaders. They would have had to get the explosives from the mining company, smuggle them into VM Major, plant them ahead of Arthur and Dwyr Orr's visit, arrange it so the security sweep overlooked them. Lots of steps. There had to be more of her followers around than only the ones who took part in the kidnapping. I did take a risk, but it was a small one." He added, "Once we were inside, it wasn't hard to get close to Arthur and he recognized us immediately."

"How could I not?" the injured king commented.

"Then, between the two of us, we easily overpowered his guards."

"I helped too!" Kayla interjected.

Taylan gave a loud sigh and shook her head again. "You were lucky more Crusaders didn't turn up."

"No chance of that," Kekoa said. "The station director put the whole place into lockdown as soon as the explosion went off. It still is, while he tries to figure out who is and isn't in the EAC."

Wright was glad to be out of that mess, but he was worried. What if Crusaders had infiltrated the security screenings to join the *Defiant*? In a few days, she would be leaving the Solar System and heading into deep space, far from Alliance help if something were to go wrong. There would be no backup, no reinforcements. If Orr attempted to take over the ship, they might not be able to stop her.

18

____

The strange man had told Setia his name was Arief but she didn't believe him. He was a liar, like Pratam. She'd sensed it in him from the beginning. But he was useful. He'd done something to her to help her fight Soleh, something she couldn't explain. Something good. She could still feel the effects even now, days later. She felt strong, capable, unbeatable. She would stick with the one who called himself Arief, at least until a better prospect came along.

Was the man he'd introduced her to a better prospect?

She couldn't tell, not yet.

She appraised him in the dark hut where they both awaited Arief's signal. The man was from another country and had an odd name: Elek.

E-lek.

She rolled the syllables quietly around her mouth.

He looked up. "Did you say something?"

"No."

Elek sat at the hut's edge, leaning his back against the wooden slats. His elbows rested on his bent knees and his forearms hung loose, like an orangutan's. His body wasn't very much different from the long-limbed ape. His height was more in his spine than his legs and his head was large, made to appear even larger by his dark curly hair and beard.

She had never seen his physical type in the flesh before. He was fifty percent larger than the average among her country-men. Wherever he went in her land he would stand out.

That was part of his appeal, Arief had explained. *In every place in these lands, people will follow you, Elek. You can do great good here. In time, you will do great good for all humanity.*

Elek's eyes had shone after Arief's speech. He must have been transported with visions of sweeping across Earth like an avenging angel, righting wrongs, bringing peace and prosperity to humankind.

Which was strange, considering things were better now than they'd ever been. The Menace in the West, the Earth Awareness Crusade, had been subdued years ago. New technology was improving everyone's lives at work and at home, medical treatments were advancing at a breath-taking pace, the environment was cleaner and greener than ever. The scientists had even mentioned they expected the climate to begin cooling and stabilizing within the next fifty years to a century.

She guessed Elek's experience of life must have been hard if he thought human civilization on Earth was in a bad way. His clothes certainly told that story. The condition of his shorts and shirt was only marginally better than her own attire, and that wasn't saying much. Threadbare sandals clung to his bony feet.

His head rose and his eyes locked on hers. "You don't need to do this, you know."

It was the first time he'd opened a conversation with her since Arief had introduced them. Their mutual acquaintance rarely left them alone together and when he did Elek spent most of the time brooding over nameless worries. She wasn't talkative herself, so the scarcity of their discussions was no wonder.

"Do what?" she asked. "Sit here with you in this stinking hut? Follow Arief's orders? Trudge around the place attending these stupid rallies?"

"You do more than attend, and you know it. It's that part I'm talking about. I am not a man of violence. I disagree with Arief's methods."

"Huh!" Setia stood and stretched her arms and back. "How far do you think you would get without me? Mobs are vicious. They can turn in an instant, and not everyone agrees with your ideas. If you didn't have someone by your side, meeting attacks with brutal defenses, you wouldn't be able to speak like you do. This isn't the West. Here, law and order are hazy, imprecise concepts. For you, I am the law."

She added, rolling her neck, "Though I'm going to suggest to Arief he recruits some more muscle. The crowds are getting bigger and there's only so much I can do, even armed."

"Yes," said Elek, brow wrinkling, "how is it you can do what you do? You don't look like a fighter."

"I think that's the point. The bullies don't expect to meet resistance when they take a swing at you. I'm usually a surprise."

"Wouldn't it make more sense to have a larger, heavier-muscled bodyguard? That would dissuade most people from attacking me."

"Perhaps, but..." She shrugged. She'd never figured that out herself so she couldn't explain it.

"I think Arief likes it," said Elek.

"Likes what?" She strode to the wall and peeked through a gap in the slats. The crowd was growing thicker and beginning to look impatient. It would be time for Elek to speak soon. She would walk with him to the podium, stand by his side while he told the people his ideas, and stick to him like glue afterward. It was usually after the speechifying, when the rally was breaking up, that a disgruntled listener would demonstrate his disagreement with what Elek had said.

"He likes it when you fight. He likes my attacker's surprise when you defend me."

She turned to look at him.

"You don't see his face," Elek continued. "You're too busy and distracted. But I've watched Arief while you're dealing with a problem. He smiles. He enjoys it."

This was news to her.

But was it so bad? Most people enjoyed seeing a good fight, especially when the person you were rooting for was winning.

"That isn't all," Elek said. "Have you noticed there's something strange about him? Do you get a funny feeling when he's around?"

She recalled the first time she'd met Arief, when Soleh had been on a mission to evict her guts from her body. Arief had appeared from nowhere. Since then, she'd convinced herself she must have missed the doorway he'd sprung from, but in truth that was unlikely. A door would have meant the difference between life and death at the time. She wouldn't have missed it. All she could remember was the sun darkening for a moment, then suddenly Arief was there.

And she couldn't deny the creepy feeling he'd given her then. The feeling had lessened over time, but spider legs still seemed to tickle her spine whenever he was near.

Elek got to his feet and walked to her side. Putting his face close to hers, he whispered, "How is it you can do what you do? How did Arief find you? Why has he put us together?"

There was something in his eyes that alarmed her. Desperation? Fear? Madness? She couldn't tell. The dimness of the hut and the way his face became shadowed as he leaned close made it hard to see him clearly.

Burnap's balls.

Mad or not, Elek was making sense. She could only fight as

well as she did because Arief had done something to her. She didn't know how or why he'd found her, nor why he'd picked her to be Elek's guardian.

He drew his head away from hers. "You won't say it, but you understand me."

The noise of the growing crowd penetrated the hut. A chant had started up.

Elek, Elek, Elek.

Other voices joined.

"If you're right," Setia said, "if there's something fishy about Arief, why are you here? Why are you letting him control you, setting up meetings and events like this?"

"I want to speak to people, lots of people, and in person. These days, everything goes on virtually. We're all just faces on a screen. It isn't meaningful. A face on a screen could be anyone, their words might not be their own. You can't tell. I want to reach people, make a connection, really make them think."

"And you need Arief to do that?"

"Since he began working for me my followers have increased exponentially. I don't know half of what he does, but whatever it is, it works for me better than anything I've ever done before."

"So you accept help from this creep you dislike and don't trust because it benefits you."

"Not me. My cause."

"But you have a problem with my presence."

"I don't know why you're here," Elek said. "I can't figure you out."

She wasn't sure why she was here either. Maybe it was because Arief had given her something she'd never had before: power. She'd always been the underling, the weak one. Trying to simply survive had meant always appeasing people stronger than you. She'd done bad things. She'd supplied drugs for users knowing they were spending money they'd stolen from their friends and family. Some of Pratam's clients had overdosed on drugs she'd given them.

Though she'd never admitted it until now, she'd hated her life. She'd hated herself.

Arief hadn't only given her a way out, he'd given her strengths and abilities she couldn't have hoped to achieve otherwise. They were heady narcotics. She was in deep.

She met Elek's gaze. "I'm here because I want to be. The same as you."

The noise of the crowd's chanting had grown so loud it almost drowned out her words.

Elek nodded, satisfied.

The door of the hut opened and Arief stood silhouetted in the frame. "It's time."

Elek strode to the entrance. As he walked out, he lifted his arms into the air.

The crowd roared.

Setia followed quietly behind.

19

Taylan smoothed medicated gel over Wright's thighs. The medic had said it was okay for him to recuperate in their cabin. He should be able to get up and walk in a couple of days, she'd said, and by this time next week his legs would be back to normal. The pulse round had only seared his skin and flesh and hadn't penetrated to the bones. It was a fortunate escape. Things could have been a lot worse in so many ways. When Taylan thought back over what had happened, her gut clenched as deadly scenarios played out in her head.

"Hey, it's all over now," Wright said gently, clearly seeing the tension on her face. "Everyone's okay."

"Yeah, you're right." She forced her mind to turn to happier things. He would get better and so would Arthur. Patrin and Kayla had received a boost to their self-esteem and a rep among the crew, and a tight lid had been sealed on Kala Orr and her son. Perhaps no one would have to set eyes on them for the entire voyage.

It would take them months to reach the area the skein mappers had suggested. Wright and she would be able to spend plenty of time together when he wasn't on duty, as there was almost nothing else to do.

Her hand moved lazily over his quads, spreading out the gel evenly, then it began to stray.

After a few moments Wright gave a small cough. "That's, er, not a wound. And while I would love to…"

She chuckled, wiped her hands clean on a towel and moved up the bed before lying down next to him, resting her head on his chest. He wrapped an arm around her.

His chest hair tickled her nose. "You know, you've never told me your real name."

"You can call me what you like. Nitwit, whatever. I don't mind."

"That's not the point. You've never told me what TJ stands for."

He was silent.

"Maybe I can guess," she said. "Is it Tyler Jacob? Trevor Jeremiah? No, it's too hard to figure out both names at the same time. I'll just try to guess your first name. Is it Thomas? Theo? Toby?"

She could hear his heartbeat quickening. She sat up. "It's one of those two, isn't it? Theo or Toby. Which one is it?"

"Taylan, leave it. It isn't important."

He looked uncomfortable and she couldn't understand why. "It's only a name. If it's embarrassing it doesn't matter. I swear I won't tell anyone. But it's weird that we're married and I don't know your name." He'd behaved oddly at their wedding, handing over the marriage document to the registrar after completing his part without allowing her to see it. "If I really want to know I only need to look up our marriage certificate. You might as well tell me."

"Then look it up," he said gruffly, turning away.

She had a sudden feeling she'd stumbled into unknown, unanticipated territory. "I-I won't if you don't want me to. Sorry

I brought it up." She lay her head on his chest once more, but he didn't put his arm over her shoulders. The mood had shifted, turning fraught and pained. She'd said something wrong, delved where she shouldn't have, and she didn't know how to get back to normality.

Wright murmured something too quietly for her to make out.

"What did you say?"

"Timbo Janus."

"What?"

Timbo Janus?!

"Don't make me repeat it a third time."

"What the hell kind of a name is that? You're kidding, right?"

His heart thudded centimeters below her ear. "Do I sound like I'm kidding?"

"Are they family names?"

"Not that I'm aware of."

"Then...why?"

Wright had told her his parents were dead. Aside from the mention of the alien masquerading as his father, he'd never mentioned them again. She knew absolutely nothing about them, except perhaps now she understood they were utter nutcases.

"I think it was a joke," he said quietly.

"Why would your parents pick a joke name for their baby?"

"I think they didn't really want a child and they wanted to punish me for my existence."

"But then why did they have you?"

"I don't know. Perhaps I was a mistake they didn't find out about until it was too late to do anything. Or maybe when the reality of parenthood hit them they changed their minds. It was all a long time ago. I don't like to talk about it."

"Bringing up kids *is* hard," she said, "even when they're

wanted and planned. I can understand when parents don't do a great job, but to give your baby a ridiculous name as a *joke* is incredibly cruel." She lifted herself up to look him in the eyes.

He wore an expression she'd never seen on him before, like a small boy's, sad and alone. Sliding her hands under his shoulders, she hugged him tightly.

"Ow," he said. "You're—"

"Sorry." She shifted away from his wounded legs. "Hey, you don't think Colbourn's like a...a..."

"What?"

"I don't want to say it."

"Come on, you can't leave me hanging. Colbourn's like a what?"

"A-a mother figure to you?"

Laughter exploded from Wright, immediately followed by groans of pain.

"Sorry," she said, trying to control her own giggles.

"Shit, Taylan. Don't do that to me."

Gradually, their mirth subsided and they lay still, not speaking.

Soon, the *Defiant* would start up her FTL engine and begin her journey, slipping along invisible pathways through the galaxy, flying at unimaginable speeds aided by her part-organic hull.

Who knew what lay ahead?

But, for now, for Taylan, she was grateful for the small respite. She was with Wright. They were together, and together they would face whatever trials the future held.

20

———————

Taylan feinted to the left. Arthur moved his shield to block the blow. At the last moment she diverted her sword's path to the right, bypassing his defense. Arthur leapt backwards, arching his torso away from the blade's point. Taylan pushed her advantage, swinging quickly out then in again, aiming for his unprotected side. Once more, her sword met empty air but it was a hair's breadth from touching him.

Another step forward and another swipe, downward this time. The point thudded into Arthur's shield. Twisting it free, she raised the blade faster than Arthur could follow. The sword neared his throat. He turned fast, too fast, and stumbled, falling to the deck, his shield flailing outward. She pinned the arm holding it under one foot, angled her blade perpendicular to Arthur's face and drove it downward. The tip hovered above his eyes.

"Ha!" Arthur exclaimed. "You killed me again. How many times is it now? Hundreds? Or maybe thousands?"

"You're thinking of Lancelot," she replied, helping him to his feet. "*I've* only killed you twenty or thirty times."

"You're right. I was forgetting. Your styles are so similar it's easy to get you two confused."

"If you know my style so well, how come you can't beat me?"

"You're too fast, and part of your style is to not be repetitive or predictable. That's hard to beat."

"If you were wielding Excalibur I'd be dead."

"Perhaps."

Arthur's sword had been a mystical gift that supposedly prevented him from receiving any mortal wounds. They were practicing with blunt weapons. Arthur refused to ever fight her with Excalibur, even in full protective gear, saying he didn't want to hurt her by mistake.

Since Merlin had reunited him with his sword he'd kept it with him always, up until his inspection tour of Valles Marineris Major, when he'd been persuaded to leave it behind. Was that why he'd been vulnerable to pulse fire and Mars's atmosphere? No one knew. Arthur's answer to the conundrum was to refuse to be parted from his weapon again. Even now, the famous blade stood propped up in a corner of the gym... where Wright now also stood, leaning a shoulder on the bulkhead, smiling as she noticed him.

"How long have you been watching us?" she asked.

"Not long."

"Witnessing another of my defeats?" asked Arthur cheerfully, clapping Wright on the shoulder as he left to change out of his gear.

"Only as a secondary effect," Wright replied. "I'm here to see Taylan."

She'd also walked across to him during the brief exchange, removing her sparring helmet. Now she'd reached him she wrapped him in her arms and kissed him.

Breaking for air, he said, "I'm not sure I'm supposed to do this while I'm on duty. In fact, I'm sure I'm not."

"I don't care."

"To be honest, I care less and less these days too. We just need to get this job done."

"I know."

"If you've finished, do you want to come with me to the Habitat?"

"Sure. Give me ten minutes."

She quickly showered and dressed.

Arthur accompanied them along the *Defiant* to the end section, which had been devoted to Iolani's green space, the zone intended to help maintain the mission members' mental health.

Taylan liked the Habitat but she hadn't been here often. Spending time with Wright and her kids brought her all the happiness she needed, for the time being anyway. She hadn't felt a need to walk the metal grid paths among lush foliage or feel the warm, moist air on her skin.

They found Iolani near the center on her knees in fresh soil, pressing a plant into place.

"Guys," she said, rising to her feet and brushing dirt from her knees, "you've come to see me? That's sweet."

"It's a semi-official visit," Wright replied. "I thought it would be fun to bring Taylan and Arthur along. How are things going around here?"

"In what sense?" she asked, somewhat warily.

"In whatever sense you think is important. Is there anything I should know?"

"Well... Let's take a walk." She led them down one of the choice of paths, apparently randomly.

Tropical trees rose overhead, their branches thick with hanging vines. Exotic flowers sprouted from nooks and crevices in their bark, and ferny undergrowth covered the ground, spilling out onto the path. They walked over rivulets and pools sparkling through the mesh holes. Taylan thought she saw the flash of silvery scales and the slither of a reptilian back.

"Are there animals here too?" she asked.

"Absolutely," replied Iolani. "Micro-organisms inhabit all living things, but the Habitat is also home to many kinds of invertebrates and vertebrates, including apex predators. Not," she added with a laugh, "anything that could hurt humans. It's a self-sustaining, self-perpetuating system, as close as I could make it. Striking the right balance is incredibly complicated. I have to check population numbers daily but that isn't too hard with the sensors. It's all worked pretty well so far. I hope things continue the same for the whole voyage."

"So does Admiral Yorkson," said Wright. "That's why he's asked me to report on how things are going."

Iolani *hmm'd* meditatively but continued to appear reluctant to speak her mind.

Taylan said, "I think I like the light best."

The lamps overhead shone brightly, casting sharp-edged shadows. The effect was as close to sunlight as she'd ever known from an artificial source. You couldn't look straight at it. Perhaps it was something to do with the new tech.

"The light is wonderful," Arthur agreed. "I almost feel as though I were back on Earth, but not my home country. These plants and this heat and moisture are strange to me."

Iolani smiled. "I'm sorry I couldn't create something more familiar for you. I had many climate types to choose from. In the end, I indulged myself and settled for the environment I grew used to in my years in Suriname."

"It's so beautiful here," said Taylan. "It must have been a wrench to leave home and go and work on a sterile starship. How did Lorcan persuade you to join the Antarctic Project? Was the salary too hard to resist?"

Iolani burst into laughter.

Taylan had a feeling she'd 'done a Kayla'. "Sorry, did I say something wrong?"

"No, it's a fair question. Let's just say Lorcan can be remarkably persuasive when he puts his mind to it."

"Oh, I can believe that."

"Here we are," said Iolani, halting.

They'd reached a junction of walkways. A path crossed theirs and they had a choice of going left or right. But Iolani turned to face them and rested her back on the guard rail in front of a multi-shaded green background. "You know what *I* love best about the place?" Not waiting for a reply, she answered her own question. "The night sky."

She must have been carrying some kind of controller because the lights rapidly dimmed until the place was utterly dark.

It was then Taylan saw the stars. "Are...is that real?"

Beyond the tree canopy hung the harsh blackness of space and the starscape. Taylan had expected the configurations to be unfamiliar—the *Defiant* was already far from the Solar System. What she hadn't been expecting was to see them *moving*. The pinpricks of light really were subtly swimming, circling, and performing other movements stars were not supposed to perform.

"It's real," Iolani confirmed. "The chief engineer... What's her name?"

"Krol," Wright supplied.

"That's it. She explained it's an effect of our passage through the skein. Nothing to be alarmed about. In fact, if you watch it for a while it's quite restful."

The four stood in silence, contemplating the strange view.

"The plants need a period of darkness to grow properly," said Iolani. "I could have just programmed regular hours for turning off the lights but I thought a night sky might help people's mental health just as much as a green environment. I asked if it was possible and, surprisingly, it was. Hey," she added apparently as an afterthought, "would you like to see—or, rather, feel—something else cool?"

"I would," Taylan replied.

"Step this way."

The stars shone sufficiently brightly to see her slip under the guard rail. Taylan did the same.

"Don't worry too much about treading on something," said Iolani. "It'll regrow." She pushed through the leaves and Taylan caught them as they sprang back.

They walked several meters over the spongy ground before she understood where Iolani was taking her. "Are we heading for the hull?"

"Exactly. But have you ever felt it?"

Taylan had not.

"This is the only place on the ship where you can actually touch it." Iolani had slowed down.

Taylan could just make out her reaching forward in the darkness. She made a soft sound of satisfaction and said, "Give me your hand."

Gently holding onto Taylan's wrist, she pulled her forward and placed her palm against something warm and moist. At first, Taylan thought Iolani had made a mistake and she was touching a peculiarly warm tree trunk, but then she sensed a flow beneath her fingertips. It was as if she had her hand on the thin, flexible skin of a warm water pipe.

"That's it?" she whispered. "*That's* the *Defiant's* hull?" She felt more than saw Iolani's nod. "Whoa."

"I know, right? It's alive."

When they returned to the walkway, Wright and Arthur were in muted conversation.

"Find something interesting?" Wright asked as Taylan climbed onto the metal gridwork.

"You could say that. You should let Iolani show you."

"Another time maybe. Iolani, what should I tell Yorkson? Everything looks good to me, but I'm not the expert here. As far as I can tell you've done a terrific job and I'm happy to report that."

"I appreciate the compliment," said Iolani, "but I'm fast coming to the conclusion this place is a complete disaster." She turned on the lights. The effect was like a swift, bright sunrise.

Wright's eyebrows popped up.

"But it's wonderful," said Taylan. "I wish I'd come here more often and brought the kids."

"That's the point," Iolani said. "Look around you. While you've been here, have you seen one other person?"

Arthur replied, "I've seen no one else."

Iolani frowned. "People come here, walk around, love it to bits, and don't come back. I'm not sure why. That's something for the psychologists to work out. But I'm worried the Habitat is having the exact opposite effect from its intention. Maybe it's *too* beautiful, too reminiscent of Earth. What if it's making the visitors more homesick than they are already?"

Wright groaned. "I see what you mean."

"When we were on the *Dauntless*," Iolani went on, "I missed green spaces so much it hurt. I really thought this place was the solution to the problems we had on that trip. Now, I think I might have been completely wrong."

"Is it really that important?" Taylan asked. "Humans have been traveling in space for centuries. We're used to it. What's the worst that can happen?"

A look passed between Iolani and Wright she couldn't fathom.

21

———————

"I have to tell them," said Taylan.

Wright heaved a sigh. "No, you don't."

It was the quiet shift and they'd just climbed into bed. The issue had been niggling at her all evening, as they'd eaten dinner, spent time with Patrin and Kayla, and while Wright had been finishing his report for Yorkson. It had been a bone of contention between them since the first day aboard ship. She'd brought up the subject over and over again, and each time Wright had shot it down, arguing there was no point now no one could change anything, that she would be de-stabilizing morale, already fragile here in the depths of interstellar space.

"But why are we on this mission?" she asked.

Wright thumped his pillow to fluff it up and replied wearily, "To challenge the aliens who have been—"

"No. Why are we *really* on this mission?"

"Umm." He lay down and put his hands, fingers linked, behind his head. "There's another reason?"

"Isn't it to stand up for what we believe in?"

"That too. Should I turn out the light?"

"In a minute. What do we believe in? What are supposed to be the Alliance's core values?"

"Taylan, it's been a long day. Can we talk about this tomorrow?"

He looked tired. From what he said, every officer-level task on the ship seemed to fall to him now he'd been promoted. And Wright *loved* his sleep. Many a time she'd marveled at how deeply he slept and how peaceful he looked—when not troubled by nightmares. She felt bad keeping him awake but she needed to follow through with this train of thought. She'd hit the essence of the problem. He had to understand her reasoning for what she was going to do.

"What are the Alliance's core values?" she repeated.

"To maintain and further human civilization and progress. To uphold basic human rights. To promote justice, truth, liberty—"

"That's right. *Truth.*"

He groaned and covered his face with a hand. "I walked right into it, didn't I?"

"How can the Alliance expect to succeed in this mission if it isn't even upholding the values it supposedly stands by?"

"The mission's success isn't going to be down to what its members know or don't know. If you go through with this you'll be causing more harm than good. I can tell you that as a fact."

"Can you? A fact? Wright, no one knows what's going to help or hinder us here. We've been picked according to some weird scientific phenomenon no one really understands, and we're traveling aboard a ship that's part tough jellyfish, off to do who knows what. There are no facts here."

He turned onto his side and propped himself up on his elbow. "You're making up justifications for something you've already decided to do. You're determined to tell them. That's what this is about."

His words hit home. "Maybe," she conceded. "Since what

happened at the Crusader festival on Ynys Môn, I feel like I owe them. They're good people and I betrayed them."

"From what you've told me, you did what you felt was right. Marc's involvement and what happened to him wasn't your fault, and you put it right the first chance you had."

She bit her lip. She'd often told herself the same kind of things but it didn't take away the guilt.

"Can we please turn out the light?" Wright asked.

She gave the command and darkness fell in their little cabin.

A muscular arm snaked out and pulled her close. Soft lips kissed her neck.

She chuckled. "I thought we were going to sleep?"

"In a little while."

THE FOLLOWING MORNING, she quickly dressed and left before Wright woke up. She didn't want to give him a chance to change her mind.

It was still early in the active shift and the passageways were empty. She'd looked up the cabin where the brothers from West BI bunked weeks ago and she remembered it off the top of her head. When she pressed the door's chime it slid open instantly without anyone asking who had come knocking.

The scene in the little space was a bustle of activity. The men had been given a four-bunk cabin though only three of them slept here. Like her and Wright, Seren and Marc had been allotted married quarters. Meilyr, Madog, and Medwyn were up and finishing their preparations to leave. Marc was already fully dressed. He stood on the other side of the doorway, open-mouthed.

"You *could* look happier to see me," she joked.

"Sorry, Taylan," he replied, breaking from his expression of surprise. "I was expecting Seren. She said she'd be here in a minute. Come in. Is everything okay? It's a little early for visitors."

"Hang on," growled Medwyn. "Don't let her in! She's here to make trouble as always."

Taylan cringed. What she was about to tell the brothers *would* make trouble. Maybe Wright was correct and she should keep her mouth shut.

Meilyr said heavily, "It's all right. That was a long time ago."

Indeed it was. Gray streaks ran through the eldest brother's hair and beard, and his siblings all showed signs of the decade that had passed since the days of the BI Resistance.

Medwyn muttered something unintelligible but, as always, conceded to Meilyr. Madog remained silent, studying her from under frowning brows.

"It won't take long," she said. "There's something I felt you deserve to know and I've come here to tell you."

The door chime sounded.

"There's Seren," said Marc.

The pretty woman stepped into the cabin and immediately paused as she took in the serious faces. "What's wrong? Has someone died?"

"Not yet," said Medwyn. "But Taylan's here so no doubt it won't be long."

She clenched her jaw. *If it hadn't been for me you could have burned innocent children alive.*

"That's not fair," said Marc.

Meilyr said, "Marc, be quiet."

"Sowing discord already," Medwyn commented. "Well done."

"Shut up," Meilyr said through his teeth. "Let her speak and get whatever it is that's bothering her off her chest, then she can go."

It pained her deeply that these people she shared so much

with—a language, culture, heritage, and, at one point, a deep comradeship—could not be her friends. But what was done was done. An expectant silence had fallen as five pairs of eyes regarded her. She took a breath. "At that first meeting after we'd boarded ship, when Yorkson announced that the skein mappers had discovered signs of the aliens' return to Earth, you, Meilyr, said the Alliance should have told us before we embarked on the mission."

"That's right," he said. "I did."

"And Yorkson replied that they didn't find out in time."

"Yes?" Meilyr was peering at her intently. Had he guessed what she was about to say?

She paused, feeling the weight of responsibility for what she was about to tell them and all the consequences she might unleash.

"It isn't true. He lied."

"I knew it!" Medwyn yelled, slamming a fist into a bunk frame.

"Are you sure?" Madog asked. "Or are you just stirring up shit again?"

"Madog's right," said Meilyr. "That's a serious allegation to make. Why should we believe you?"

"Wait." Medwyn got up close and thrust his face into hers. "You're trying to weasel your way in with us again, aren't you? Pretending you're on our side. Telling us lies to make us think you're our friend."

"For stars' sake," said Marc, pulling him back. "Knock it off. What makes you think Taylan would want to be *your* friend, you pock-marked, middle-aged moron?"

"Get your hands off me, little brother. Everyone knows you always had a thing for her. Sorry, Seren, but it's true."

The young woman's gaze was traveling from brother to brother with a look of bewilderment. "You're all mad, except for Marc. What kind of family have I married into? You're forgetting Taylan and I already know each other. We met in the Resistance days. I didn't see much of her but I saw enough to know she isn't a troublemaker. She's brave, loyal, and honest. If you want to find out the cause of the strife between you, look to yourselves."

"*Please*," said Taylan, "just hear me out. I'll explain how I know Yorkson was lying and then you can judge for yourselves. I'm only here because my knowledge of the truth has been eating away at me for weeks. We've had our differences—"

Medwyn gave a snort of derision. "You can say that again."

Ignoring him, she continued, "But I respect you guys. *All* of you, even if I don't get it back. Maybe I don't deserve it." She went on to tell them about her and Wright's visit to the Institute of Skein Studies and how Colbourn had spoken to Wright separately. "After that, he was *very* insistent that I and my kids joined the mission."

"But he didn't know how long he would be gone," said Seren. "He didn't want to leave you behind."

"It was that too," Taylan admitted, "but I've asked him since if he found out about the aliens' return that day and he hasn't denied it."

"He hasn't confirmed it either?" asked Marc.

"I know him," said Taylan. "If I was wrong he would tell me. Our visit to the institute was months before the mission departure date. They knew. The Alliance knew and they didn't tell you, not until you were safely aboard ship and there was no going back."

22

———————

In the months that had passed since the *Defiant* had departed Mars orbit, Kala Orr's anger had built to screaming pitch. She'd complained, sent in requests for a hearing, and regularly demanded to speak to Yorkson, but she'd been completely ignored. The glaringly obvious injustice of her position was apparently only clear to her. No matter how much she objected, the Alliance insisted on treating her like a common criminal. Her, the Dwyr! Even Perran didn't share her opinion about their outrageous treatment, despite the fact that he had to be suffering too.

She'd laid it out to him countless times.

It's entirely normal and expected that we should try to resume control. We can't be blamed for it.

The BA has stripped us of all our rights and dignity. Who wouldn't want to do something about it?

The Alliance has to understand we couldn't take their insults lying down.

A reasonable period of punishment is to be expected, but to incarcerate us both for the whole voyage, there and back, is outrageous. Animals are treated better than this.

The few times Perran voiced a reply to her comments, it was always along the lines of separating himself from inclusion in her actions: *I hate it when you say 'we'. It was* you *who did it all, Mother. You dragged me into your schemes, and now I'm paying the price.*

The worst thing about the fury coursing through her veins was it had no outlet. In her previous life, when the Crusade dominated all of Europe and was working its way across the globe, in times of great stress she would go to a high tower facing the sea and whip the tension from her body. As the blood flowed her feelings would ease. Here in this loathsome cabin there was nothing she could use for a similar relief. Everything with which she might harm herself had been removed and cameras watched them constantly.

It was unbearable.

Perran passed the time by *painting*. Her son, painting! Like some sniveling, weak-willed, lackluster underdog. He'd been working on this latest picture for days. An abstract painting, swirls of deep purple, gray, and black swept across the surface. What did it mean? He would never explain his work, only saying it was up to the observer to take whatever they wanted from it.

Sometimes, she doubted she understood him at all.

Despite sensing the act was desperate and futile, she scribbled a note on a piece of paper. Writing something down was the only way to avoid the Alliance's scrutiny. The watchers would see that she'd written, but not what she wrote, and after Perran had read her words she could destroy the evidence.

She poked his back.

Sighing, he put down his brush and turned. "Mother, I..." He'd spotted what was in her hand. "Ugh, not *again*."

"Read it," she hissed. "Just read it."

"There's no point—"

"I am your mother and the Dwyr."

His expression twisted in disgust but he took the proffered paper.

She knew the message off by heart now. She'd made the proposal several times.

Tell the guard you need psychiatric help, that you're going crazy trapped in here day after day. Tell her you're having suicidal thoughts. That's all you need to do. I can do the rest.

The ploy had worked once. On the *Dauntless*, she'd managed to fool the idiot psychiatrist and secure some small freedoms. But the same trick wouldn't work for her again, not even on the stupid Alliance admiral. But he might believe Perran. She suspected the Alliance trusted him more. He'd been under their sway for years in her absence. They were probably only keeping him imprisoned with her as a precaution, not because they believed he was her conspirator in the events at Mars Station. They didn't want her to have any influence on anyone outside her place of incarceration, and being her son made Perran vulnerable.

He had given her note a cursory glance. Now he was looking at her, exasperation written over his features. "How many times do I have to tell you I refuse to go along with your little ruses? I won't do it, Mother. I simply won't do it. And not only that..." He folded the paper neatly in half, turned, and marched toward the other side of the cabin.

Realizing where he was headed, she exclaimed, "No, Perran, no! Don't do that." She raced to his side and attempted to snatch the paper out of his hand.

He simply lifted it up into the air. He was a lanky young man, and easily moved the note out of her reach.

She thought of another tactic. She darted ahead of him. When she reached the garbage chute, she about-faced and covered it with her back, spreading her arms out. "If you put it in there they'll collect it and read it. They'll know what I was trying to do."

"Mother, they already know what you're trying to do. You demonstrated your intentions very effectively on Mars. I don't even need to put this note in the disposal. I could hold it up to one of the cameras. Should I do that instead?"

"You wouldn't!"

"Wouldn't I?"

She covered her face with her hands. "Don't you care anything about me? You and I are all we have in the world. We should care for each other. Why won't you do this tiny thing for me?"

"Because we're in enough trouble as it is. Every time you pull a stunt like you did on Mars and get caught, I'm tarred with the same brush. It isn't fair. I just want to live a normal life. I don't want to be the Dwyr's son. I don't want to belong to a weird cult."

She threw down her hands and clenched them into fists, hissing, "The Crusade is not a *weird cult*." Marching away from the chute, she continued, "How I rue the day I released Morgan from her underground prison. That was the point at which everything began to go wrong. She took over my life, took my son from me, ruined everything."

"No. *You* ruined everything. You ruined everything for me. You made me a nasty brat. You were hardly ever there, leaving me to be brought up by servants, and when you were there you spoiled me, puffing me up with ideas of my own importance. It took a long time for me to understand it but years of living a normal life made it clear in the end. You were a terrible parent and I'm still suffering the consequences. Besides, your downfall had nothing to do with Morgan. It was Arthur's return that turned the tide for the Alliance."

His ingratitude and criticism washed over her like burning oil. She could only splutter, "That's what they want you to believe. You shouldn't listen to the propaganda. I was there. I know what happened. You were only a child, and Morgan had turned you against me by then."

"I liked her. She paid more attention to me than you ever did."

"How dare you!" Kala whipped around and raised a hand to slap Perran's face.

But he caught her forearm in mid-air. His grip was surprisingly powerful. He squeezed her muscle and forced her arm down. Leaning in, he whispered, "Don't even *think* about it, Mother. I am not a child anymore, and I won't put up with your bullying. Nor will I take part in your ridiculous plans. Your time is over. You're a has-been, a nothing." He put his lips close to her ear and hissed, "You're pathetic."

He let go of her arm and she collapsed to the deck. Against her will, sobs erupted from her throat. She sprawled on her front, despair, shame, and humiliation consuming her.

23

Yorkson had called a meeting. Wright didn't know exactly why. Colbourn hadn't told him anything, and the reason for the meeting was vague: to address issues arising aboard the ship. The notice given was short, only an hour and a half, and attendance was mandatory for everyone except for a skeleton crew. He could see Taylan, Patrin, and Kayla in the crowded space but the seats adjoining them were already occupied. He found one of the few empty ones and sat down.

When the meeting started, it wasn't Yorkson who walked to the front, it was Dr Kim, while the admiral quietly took up a position behind her. Wright knew the psychiatrist well from his previous dealings with her aboard the *Dauntless*. For this trip, she'd left him alone so far.

"Thank you all for coming," the doctor said. "I apologize for dragging you away from your activities, but I have an announcement that I felt was more appropriate to make face to face rather than as an impersonal comm." She paused and then said gravely, "It is with great sadness I have to inform you that Lance Corporal Buchanan died by his own hand today."

She waited as murmurs of shock and sadness ran through the audience.

Wright cursed and put his head in his hands. He knew the man, of course, though not well. Buchanan had worked on the bridge, relaying and interpreting sensor data. He had always completed his duties skillfully and efficiently, never giving the slightest trouble to his superior officers. Wright couldn't remember noticing any signs of distress in him. He'd hidden his feelings well.

"Naturally," the doctor said, "this is devastating news, the last thing any of us wants to hear. For anyone who wishes to pay their last respects, his funeral will take place tomorrow at 1200 hours at Airlock B. His family has been informed."

Yet again, she paused, surveying the assemblage. "This event is not only appalling for Buchanan's friends and associates, it also has wide-ranging implications for the rest of the ship's personnel. His superior officers may feel they failed him, and that is a burden I and the rest of the psychiatric team carry too, irrationally. He had not approached any of us regarding his mental state. Unfortunately, failure to seek treatment is a common symptom of depression and anxiety as well as, if I may say, the military mindset. Admitting you may be suffering from mental ill health while in military service is sometimes seen as weak and shameful, whereas in fact it is nothing of the kind."

She sighed and said, "I digress. Some of you here are veterans of the voyage of the *Dauntless* and are aware of the similar problems we experienced on that mission. Buchanan's death must be a wake-up call to us all. According to updates we've received from skein mappers on Earth, we are still some distance from our destination. We must do all we can to prevent further events. I would ask that if you feel you or someone you know may need help, to please, please, please contact the psychiatric team. Whatever the hour, there will always be someone available. Thank you."

She stepped away from the central position and Yorkson took her place.

"Thank you, Dr Kim. Needless to say, I will be personally expressing my deepest sorrow and sympathies to Lance Corporal Buchanan's parents. Now, as our mission continues, it is beholden upon all of us to do everything we can to maintain morale and a positive outlook. Therefore, as well as taking away the sad news from this gathering today, I would ask you to think of suggestions to improve the mood aboard ship. We already have the Habitat. I encourage you to visit it whenever you can. Green spaces are good for mental health. What else can we do? We need distractions and activities to strengthen our community."

A hand went up. "Permission to speak, sir." It was an officer cadet, probably the youngest Marine on board, not much older than Patrin.

"Granted."

The Marine stood and addressed the audience. "Anyone who likes playing board games is welcome to join the xiangqi tournament. It's a tough game but a lot of fun. I'm sure Abacha won't mind people joining late."

"Not at all," Abacha said. "I'm happy to explain the rules to newbies."

"At length," drawled an anonymous voice, drawing a ripple of gentle laughter that eased the tense, melancholic mood.

Arthur also rose to his feet. The king did not seek Yorkson's permission to speak. "Taylan Ellis and I are well-versed in ancient fighting arts. We are happy to provide demonstrations and practice sessions."

Taylan turned and locked gazes with Wright, her expression saying everything about Arthur blithely volunteering her without consultation.

"That is an excellent idea, Your Majesty," said Yorkson. "I'm sure there are many among our military and civilian divisions who would be interested in taking up your offer."

As Arthur sat down, Meilyr stood up.

What would his suggestion be? Perhaps he might teach his native language. If so, Wright considered attending lessons. He was interested to learn but Taylan always put him off, telling him she had enough to do already.

But the man from West BI had a face full of thunder. "Well, isn't this all lovely? A man kills himself and the Alliance seizes the chance to create a bit of community feeling."

Yorkson said, "I'm not sure what your point is, but this isn't the time or place—"

"It's *exactly* the time and place. I've been waiting until most of us were gathered together again to say my piece."

Shit.

She's told them.

For months, Taylan had been threatening to spill the beans to her countrymen. She'd gone and done it.

Meilyr leveled a pointed finger at Yorkson. "You, sir, are a liar."

The admiral's eyes flicked to the two entrances to the auditorium, where, in a more formal situation, guards would stand.

There were no guards.

Meilyr continued, speaking generally to those seated around him, "When we boarded this ship we all attended a meeting similar to this, where we were informed that the aliens who are the targets of this mission had already returned to Earth. They were walking among us again, playing their games with human lives. We were told this information was new, that it had arrived too recently to tell the mission members and let them make their own decisions about whether to leave their loved ones behind. That was a lie." He swept his gaze back to Yorkson. "Wasn't it."

The admiral didn't answer.

Dr Kim stepped forward. "Whatever your complaint is, there are channels through which you can make it. Hijacking this meeting for your own purposes is inappropriate, especially considering the reason we're all here in the first place."

"What? You think my point isn't relevant to that young man's death? Doctor, it has everything to do with it. While we've been gone, years have passed on Earth. I don't know who among you still watches the news reports. I know I find it hard to myself. It makes me too conscious of the life and people I left behind. It makes me feel like everything's moved on without me. But I do watch them. Things have been happening back home that worry me. They make me fear for the future of everyone I care about. If I'd known I would be in this position, I would never have left. But I had my decision taken from me by that man." He pointed again. "And if *that* isn't a morale-killer, I don't know what is. So enjoy your little games and play-fighting. I and my brothers will have no part of it. From now on, we won't be participating in this mission because we are not here of our free will. Until we return to Earth, we will be unwilling passengers on this ship, just waiting to disembark."

He pushed past the people sitting in his row, moving toward the aisle. At this signal, Medwyn, Madog, and Marc also rose. Meilyr marched to the exit and his brothers followed, though Marc gave Taylan an apologetic glance.

When the door had slid closed behind them, Yorkson spoke into the shocked silence. "I apologize for that man's outburst. I have absolutely no idea what he was talking about. It may be he's in the throes of a mental health crisis." He asked Kim, "Perhaps you or someone from your team could speak to him?"

"Certainly, Admiral."

24

____

Brigadier Colbourn stared at Wright for so long without saying anything he began to grow uncomfortable. He knew why she wanted to speak to him. He wished she would get it over with.

Things had been going so well too, everything considered. Taylan and he were getting along great. The kids were still enjoying the voyage and hadn't yet realized how monotonous and boring space travel really was. Buchanan's death was a tragedy, but, generally, morale seemed better this time compared to the _Dauntless_. For one thing, there were no pale ghosts appearing at random. That always helped.

"Is this mission a joke to you, Lieutenant-Colonel?"

"I'm sorry, ma'am?" He squirmed in his seat, facing her across her desk. Despite all the years he'd known her—or maybe because he knew her so well?—Colbourn had a knack for making him feel like a naughty schoolboy.

"I'll put it more simply," Colbourn said icily, rising from her seat. "Do you think we're all here for fun? Is this voyage a jaunt? A jolly jape? A light-hearted prank to tickle the fancy of the aliens plaguing humanity?" As she'd spoken, she leaned a little farther over her desk with each example she gave.

He gritted his teeth. His superior officer's anger might be justified, but he was no grunt. He was a Royal Marine officer. "Ma'am, if you want to talk about Meilyr's outburst, I would appreciate it if you would get to the point."

"Hmpf!" Glaring at him, she sat down. "I have to say, ever since you became involved with that woman your standards have slipped."

"I don't understand."

"There's no nice way to put this. Your behavior and attitude have become impaired."

"No," he said, forcefully. "What I don't understand is how you dare to refer to my wife as *that woman*."

She locked gazes with him.

He stared back, unblinking.

She broke eye contact. "You're correct. I *have* requested a meeting with you in order to discuss the breach of security that resulted in today's debacle." Knitting her fingers, she rested her elbows on the desktop. "Only a very few Royal Marine officers were made aware of the skein mappers' findings and the increase in urgency for the mission. Neither Yorkson nor I can think of a reason any of those officers would have divulged the information to civilians on this ship. Such an action would be extremely foolish. It would incite discontent and dissent, as we saw happen today. Not only would it be foolish, it would be a direct contravention of orders."

She paused. When he didn't speak, she asked, "Do you have anything to say?"

"Do you mean in terms of, if I confess my lapse I won't face a court martial?"

"Something like that, perhaps. We'll have to see. Wright, it's clear the breach must have come from you. Taylan Ellis, your wife, is friends with those men from West BI. They were in the

Resistance together. Even if we didn't have their connection through the skein, it's all documented. There's only one conclusion to draw. You told Ellis, and Ellis told Meilyr. If you admit to it, things might go marginally easier for you when we return to Earth."

"Might go marginally easier? Wow, I must take up that offer."

"Sarcasm won't help you." Colbourn sighed and passed a hand over her eyes. "What happened to you? You used to be a fine officer. When we served on the *Dauntless*, I really thought you'd turned a corner. I said to myself, *At last. The old Wright is back again.* Then Ellis returns to the scene and you fall apart. She's just a woman. I don't understand why she has such a profound influence over you."

"Clearly." He actually felt sorry for Colbourn. She was wedded to the Alliance. She was a spouse of military service. She really didn't understand human relationships. "Brigadier, I can see how you might find it difficult to believe, but I didn't tell Taylan or Meilyr that we knew about the aliens' return well before the start of the mission."

"You're right. I do find that difficult to believe."

"If I can explain?"

She gave a cautious nod.

He related the basics, about how the meeting where she'd told him the Alliance suspected the aliens were back had taken place during Taylan and her family's visit to the Institute, and how Taylan had gone on to put two and two together. "She isn't stupid, Brigadier. She might not act like it sometimes, but she's very smart. When she asked me about what you'd told me that day, I couldn't deny it. I can't and won't lie to her. I know you don't get it, but she means everything to me. My relationship with her is more important than my service. It's more important than anything."

Colbourn's look was full of pity. "You poor, deluded man. I

can see she's thrown a spell over you more powerful than any of Kala Orr's prestidigitations."

"Deluded or not, I didn't contravene any orders and I wasn't responsible for a security breach. It's all an unfortunate coincidence of events."

"*If* I believe you, it absolutely is not."

"Why?"

"Even if *you* didn't tell Meilyr, Ellis did. She deliberately passed on sensitive intelligence, entirely heedless of the consequences."

"And what are you going to charge her with? She isn't a Royal Marine."

"She signed a security contract."

"So did Meilyr and his brothers. She passed information to people at the same security clearance level as her. And it wasn't even information. It was a guess that happened to be right."

"Nevertheless, her actions have resulted in anger, disruption, and turmoil aboard this ship at a crucial point in our mission. You remember what happened on the *Dauntless*? Do you want to see a repeat?"

Wright leaned against his seatback and folded his hands in his lap. "Is all this really Taylan's fault? Isn't it the Alliance's?"

"How so?"

"We withheld crucial information from the mission members. I'm sorry, Brigadier, but I happen to think Meilyr's anger is justified. He and all the other civilians should have been informed about the mappers' findings. The Alliance behaved badly and now we're suffering the results."

Colbourn tutted and shook her head. "I don't know what's got into you, Wright. I really don't."

LATER, when he returned to his cabin, Taylan greeted him at the door with a hug. "Was it bad? Did she tear strips off you? Have you been demoted?"

"It was fine," he replied, hugging her back. "Don't worry about it."

25

Teaching ancient fighting techniques turned out to be more enjoyable than Taylan had anticipated. Kevin had taken up Arthur's offer and so had a man Wright served with on the *Resolute*: Captain Ford. It was nice to see more of Kevin and she enjoyed listening to the two men's accents. It reminded her of her time in Australia and finally finding Patrin and Kayla.

Kevin was one of the few civilians who attended the sessions. Most of the participants were military, including—to her delight—Abacha. She hadn't managed to spend much time with him yet. She missed their late-night xiangqi sessions, even though she'd lost every match, and the friendship of her bunkmate during a tough time in her life. She'd been self-sabotaging then, punishing herself for abandoning her search for her kids.

The training sessions were so popular she'd drafted in Patrin to help. He was as good as her at most of the techniques now, if not better in some things, and he had height and weight to use to his advantage, which he did to great effect. Teaching him as he grew up had been a bittersweet process, reminding her of Dad and how he must have felt when passing on his skills to her. At the time, she hadn't been aware of the pride and joy you experienced when your kid learned something new or improved their expertise.

She and Arthur kept the format simple. They began each session with a short demonstration, followed by an explanation of what they'd done and why. Sometimes they would break down moves into their component parts and slowly replay them step by step. Then the group would split into pairs to practice and Taylan and Arthur would observe and give tips and advice. Finally, the bravest pairs would take turns to step up to the front and spar.

It was a lot of fun and the participants seemed to enjoy themselves too.

Patrin turned eighteen on a training day, and Taylan arranged a surprise celebratory dinner in the mess. It wouldn't be a typical eighteenth-birthday bash, but there wouldn't be many eighteen-year-olds who could say their party took place aboard a starship in interstellar space.

Kevin and Patrin were the last pair to spar at the end of the day's session. Kevin had taken to calling Patrin 'nipper', which was hilarious considering the boy stood head and shoulders taller than the Australian. He'd taken some persuading to believe that Patrin was the little boy he'd helped to find in the outback.

"All right, nipper," he drawled as they squared up. "Show me what you got."

The audience chuckled.

"Go easy on him, Kevin," Ford called out. "Y' don't wanna embarrass the kid."

Laughter echoed around the gym. Most of those present had fought Patrin or had seen him fight. No one was in any doubt about which of the two would be embarrassed.

Patrin smiled good-naturedly. He lifted his sword.

Kevin did the same and also raised his shield.

"Remember, Patrin," said Taylan, lifting her voice over the audience's chatter. "Focus. Don't let anything distract you." Once, long ago it seemed, when she'd been sparring at staves with Arthur, Merlin had clapped loudly and broken her concentration. The result had been a smashed-in nose. She'd been careful to help her son avoid making a similar mistake.

Boy and man began to circle, gazes locked.

Kevin broke first, darting in to slash at Patrin's knees. The boy batted the blade away with the part of his sword nearest the hilt—the forte—like a man brushing a fly from his face. Kevin drew back, and they circled again.

Kevin's best hope against an opponent with a longer reach was to get in close where reach didn't matter, but sword-fighting up close was awkward and clumsy, and Patrin would try to avoid it if he could. Yet, as Taylan watched, he didn't really seem to be trying. With his height, weight, and skill superiority, he could drive forward and finish Kevin off in a couple of blows. He was kindly allowing the man time to practice and letting him save face.

Kevin tried again. He bounded forward and smashed his shield into Patrin's. The force merely made the boy rock a little on his heels. Kevin swiped with his sword, but Patrin had anticipated the blow and deflected it with his guard.

Taylan mentally followed through what should happen next. Kevin's left side was open. All Patrin had to do was angle his sword toward Kevin's throat and poke upward. But he didn't. He leaned his shoulder into his shield and forced the Australian backward, creating space between them once more.

"It's like a cat playing with a mouse," came a quiet remark. "Painful to watch."

Kevin didn't hang around before launching his third attack. He raced at Patrin, clashing shields with him again. This time, he tried to stab across his body at Patrin's leg, but again the boy guessed the trajectory of the blade and smoothly turned to the side. He collided with Kevin, unbalancing him. Before he could recover, Patrin hooked his foot behind the older man's ankle, re-doubling his downward motion.

Then Kevin was on the deck and the point of Patrin's sword was at his throat.

Clapping broke out in the audience.

Kevin clambered to his feet and tucked his sword under his shield arm to shake Patrin's hand. "Happy birthday, fella."

The boy's eyes widened and he looked at Taylan. The time for subterfuge was over. She told him to get changed and come to the mess.

Wright joined them for the party, sitting down next to her as the cook and helpers brought the food out. Abacha sat on her other side. Patrin was guided to the head of the table, the guest of honor. He looked embarrassed, but a little embarrassment wouldn't hurt. He would only turn eighteen once.

The cooks had prepared his favorite foods, including leek pie made from a crop Iolani had been surreptitiously growing for months in a specially cooled section of the Habitat. Beer was also served. As Patrin drank his serving, Taylan turned to Wright and asked, "Did you see that?"

"Hm? What?"

"This isn't the first time he's drunk beer."

Wright shrugged. "What did you expect? How old were you when you had your first drink?"

She colored before replying, "That was different."

Wright gave her a sideways hug and then continued to shovel food into his mouth.

She asked, "There isn't going to be any hazing, is there? I've heard about what can happen in the military on birthdays."

"No way," Wright replied through a mouthful of food. "Patrin isn't a Royal Marine, and even if he were it would be a brave man who would try anything with him."

The guests had brought presents—small, simple gifts

they'd created, re-purposed, or printed. T-shirts, a shaving kit, cakes and candies, a comb, a holoscribe. Taylan was grateful. She hadn't managed to find anything to give him. Instead, she'd promised that when they returned to Earth they would go shopping for something special.

Arthur got up from his seat and walked to Patrin's, drawing everyone's attention. Though they were all used to his presence, he remained King of the Britannic Isles. He handed Patrin a gift wrapped in plain paper.

When Patrin tore the paper open, gold glinted from within it. A hush settled over the table. Patrin pulled out Arthur's arm torc.

His eyes round, he stared at Taylan and then Arthur. "I can't accept this." He tried to force the torc into the king's hands.

Arthur gently pushed it back. "You must. You are a warrior now. In my time, I would have made you a knight of my table, and it would have gladdened my heart to have you among their company."

Turning to Taylan again, he asked, "Mam?"

She shrugged. "He's the king. You have to do what he says."

His expression a picture of pride and joy, Patrin slipped the torc over his sleeve and up his arm until it clung to his biceps.

Arthur clapped him on the shoulder before returning to his seat.

Kayla rose to her feet and tapped her glass with a fork until she had everyone's attention.

"What's this about?" Wright quietly asked.

"I've no idea," replied Taylan. "It isn't in the timetable."

What was her daughter going to say? Taylan held her breath.

Kayla said, "As no one is giving a speech…" she looked pointedly at Taylan "…I suppose I'd better. I'd like to wish my brother a very happy birthday. He's a very nice brother, even though he can be annoying sometimes. But even if I had the chance, I wouldn't change him. I like the one I've got. What some of you might not know..." she cast her gaze up and down the table "...is that Patrin and I were kidnapped by Crusaders when we were much younger. I was so little I don't really remember anything about it. But what I do remember is that Patrin was always there for me. When I was hungry he gave me his food, and when I was tired he carried me on his back."

The party mood was evaporating, replaced by poignancy.

Kayla, in her typical way, continued blithely without noticing the change in atmosphere. "I was only three or four years old. I can't imagine what it must have been like for him, just a young boy as he was then, to be responsible for me and keep me safe. But he did it. And he doesn't remind me about it every day like some brothers would. He never talks about it at all. *We* never talk about it. So I want to take this chance to say thank you, big brother, for saving my life, and I love you."

Patrin's chin trembled and he nodded. Taylan ran her fingertips under her eyes but the tears flowed anyway. She also exhaled in relief. Kayla hadn't put her foot in it like she usually did.

Kayla went on, addressing the table, "Now we just need to get this mission over so we can go home. Patrin has never had a girlfriend, you see, and he should get one now he's grown up." She sank abruptly into her seat.

Gasps and titters ran around the room and Patrin turned beet red.

Wright shot to his feet and raised his glass. "A toast to Patrin! Happy birthday!"

"Happy birthday," the guests echoed on cue and took a drink.

Four late arrivals entered the mess and heads swiveled toward them.

Marc walked up to Taylan and bent down to whisper in her

ear. "We would like to come to the party if that's all right. If you'd rather we didn't, we'll understand."

"Of course you can join us," she replied. "Of course. Where's Seren?"

"She's on her way."

Medwyn didn't look too happy about being here, but Meilyr and Madog sent her apologetic smiles as people shuffled up to make room for them and found extra seats.

Her heart swelled. The peace gesture was very welcome.

26

Patrin got over his embarrassment at Kayla's announcement—aided in part by several glasses of beer—and celebrations continued into the quiet shift. By the time the party was over, nearly everyone had shown their face. Iolani tore herself away from her precious Habitat for a few hours, and even Colbourn and Yorkson put in an appearance, though, Taylan guessed, that was probably to ensure no one drank too much. The only two people who didn't turn up at some point couldn't and no one would have wanted them to anyway. Taylan hadn't seen Kala Orr or her son since the encounter at Mars Station, and if she never saw them again it would be too soon.

Wright fell into a tipsy sleep as soon as his head hit the pillow, and Taylan soon followed him, slipping into slumber contentedly.

It seemed only minutes later the door chime woke her.

She padded across the dark room to see who it was. Kayla's sad, tearful face appeared on the panel.

Had she realized she'd embarrassed her brother at his party?

"Mam, I had a nightmare."

Glancing at Wright, who hadn't stirred at all from his usual comatose state, Taylan opened the door.

"Can I come in?" Kayla asked, a catch in her voice.

"Uhh...I'll come to your room."

Somehow, Kayla had managed to increase her wardrobe exponentially during the months she'd spent aboard the ship. The clothes were predictably strewn all over her cabin and Taylan had to pick her way through them to reach Kayla's bed.

The girl was so distraught by her dream she didn't make even a half-hearted effort to tidy up. "Oh, Mam." She plonked herself on her bunk. "I had a dream about Carys."

"Lie down," Taylan said. "Tell me about it." She cuddled Kayla from behind.

"I dreamt she'd climbed onto one of her birds of prey and it was flying away with her. I called out but she didn't hear me. She didn't look back, no matter how loud I shouted. And then she was gone."

"That sounds more sad than scary. Do you miss her?"

"I miss her so much, Mam. And I miss all my friends. I found out today Mikaela got married." She quietly wept. "It was someone else who told me. Mikaela doesn't talk to me anymore."

Mikaela had been Kayla's best friend. During the months of travel on the *Defiant*, years had passed on Earth. Kayla's friend had grown up and become a woman. She probably couldn't relate to a teenage girl now. It was sad but it couldn't be helped. Taylan guessed Kayla's dream had something to do with the news.

The usual time dilation formula didn't apply, though the physicists didn't understand why yet. Traveling through passages within the skein complicated things. Regardless, the upshot was time passed at home much faster than it did on the ship, sometimes at unpredictable rates.

Where was Carys? What was she doing? They'd received their last message from her not long after they'd set off and she didn't answer Taylan's comms. Had she found it too painful to continue the relationship? Whatever the reason, Taylan didn't blame her. Kayla hadn't mentioned her in the party speech, but Carys was just as responsible for Kayla's survival as her brother was. Carys had kept them alive in the desert for days while Taylan searched for them. She would forever be in her debt and would never forget her.

She recalled one of the last times she'd seen her adopted daughter.

They'd gone as a family to see a raptor display held at the rescue center where Carys worked. The event was a regular fund-raiser and it was to be her first time presenting.

As they waited for the display to be set up, Taylan slid along the bench, moving close to Wright.

He put his arm around her. "Are you cold?"

"No, I'm fine."

The crowd hummed and bustled, taking their seats.

He asked, "Are you having second thoughts about the mission?"

"My whole life is a second thought at the moment, but, no, I agreed we would go and we will."

"That doesn't mean you have to like it, though, right?"

"Right." She sighed, nestling her head into his shoulder. "I wish Carys was coming too. I'm going to miss her. So will the kids. She's been a part of the family for years. But she isn't a child any longer, she's her own person. If she wasn't so mature and capable, I'd argue harder with her about her decision."

"A hard upbringing will do that to you," Wright said. "And they don't come much harder than being brought up in a cult. Patrin and Kayla were lucky to get out while they were still young."

Taylan silently agreed.

He continued, "Carys doesn't figure in the connections that bind the rest of us."

"I know, but..." Her words faltered to silence. There were more connections in life than the ones the skein mappers identified.

The announcer walked out into the ring and the crowd's chatter quickly ceased.

Kayla's voice broke into the quiet. "Is Carys on first?"

Patrin elbowed her.

"Yes," Taylan whispered, "she's on first."

Her adopted daughter stepped into the ring, a falcon on her wrist. She greeted the crowd and then explained the bird she carried was called Sparky and he was a merlin.

"Glad it's not the other kind," Wright muttered.

The merlin leapt into the air and flew over the audience's heads, bells on its jesses jangling. The crowd gasped and a few people ducked. The bird landed on a pole at the back of the stadium and perched there, blinking in the morning light. Carys took a small piece of meat from a bag at her hip and grasped it between her finger and thumb, holding it up for the bird to see.

"In a minute," she said, "the sun will disappear behind that cloud, a wind will rise, and then Sparky will swoop down for his breakfast."

Kayla said, "Carys is doing really well, isn't she, Mam?"

"She's doing great."

Exactly as Carys had predicted, the sky darkened, a breeze started up, and down came Sparky, sweeping low.

It had been a beautiful day, a wonderful final family gathering.

Kayla's chest was rising and falling steadily. She was asleep.

An idea suddenly hit, and tears slid from Taylan's eyes.

Had Kayla's dream been an omen?

She had an awful feeling she would never see Carys again.

27

———

"What do you think about joining the Antarctic Project?" Setia asked Elek. "There's still time but we'll have to be quick. The final deadline for applications is tomorrow. It's expensive but you must be able to afford it. You make even more than me at this game. The first ship leaves in six months."

He looked up from his meal. "Are you serious? Why would I want to do that?"

"You know why."

"Do I?"

Exasperated, Setia placed the interface heavily on the cafe table. The jerky movement and accompanying sound of impact attracted curious glances from some of the diners. Ordinarily, the ones who hadn't recognized Elek yet would have risen from their seats and walked over, eager to meet the leader of the fastest-growing movement in the southern hemisphere. But they were in a new place, a country that hadn't been exposed to Elek's oratory or Arief's publicity machine. The diners who had stopped their conversations to check out the small disturbance returned their attention to their companions.

"Yes," she insisted, "you do."

Did she have to spell it out? It looked like he was going to make her.

She liked Elek. The same as most people, she found it impossible not to. In the years since they'd met they'd grown close and even had a brief, mutually unsatisfactory, sexual relationship. But sometimes he was infuriating.

"It isn't safe to carry on like this," she said. "It was fun in the beginning, I admit. I liked being your bodyguard and destroying the knuckle-draggers. And, let's face it, you loved all the attention. That was then. This is now. Things have changed. What you're doing isn't safe anymore. Not for anyone."

"What *I'm* doing?" Elek lazily lifted a forkful of his rice-and-bean dish to his mouth. Before popping it in, he said, "I thought we were in this together."

She watched as he chewed. "I don't know where you get that idea. Arief asked me to help you. Signing up to your cause wasn't part of the deal. I'm not one of your followers."

He smirked and swallowed.

"You're teasing me," she said. "I'm being serious."

"Sorry, Setia. I couldn't resist. I know you don't believe in half of what I say, and in fairness that's refreshing. Unquestioning adoration can get boring. I like having you around."

"Then think about what I'm telling you or you might not have me around for much longer."

"Arief might have something to say about that."

"Arief can go suck on..." Frustration had made her voice loud. The other diners had grown interested again. She leaned over the table and said at a quieter volume, "...Burnap's balls. My life is my own, whatever Arief might want."

"You say that a lot. I've always wondered who Burnap is and what his testicles have to do with anything."

"Burnap is a deity in my religion. A god—like you want to become."

Elek frowned. "You have me wrong. I don't want to be a god. My aim is to empower people so they don't feel the need to obey any gods. I want them to become masters of their own destinies."

Setia lifted an eyebrow. "By getting them to follow you?"

"I don't want them to follow, only listen."

Coming from anyone else, Elek's words might have sounded ironic. But he was in earnest. Something she'd come to understand about him was when he said things like that, he really believed it. He was a slave to attention from others but only because he felt he had an important message. He wanted to help people. When she'd said his goal was to become a god, she'd meant he wanted people to follow his creed, intended to make them happier and fulfilled in their lives.

She rubbed her temples with her fingertips to ease the headache beginning to form. "I know you're sincere. If you weren't, I wouldn't help you. It certainly isn't for Arief's sake. But what's happening—what we're doing—it's getting dangerous."

Elek's mouth turned down and he pushed away his half-finished plate. "You're talking about what happened at the last rally."

"Isn't it obvious? What else could I be talking about?"

At his most recent event a combination of high temperatures and the organizers allowing too many people in had sparked a stampede. Five attendees had been crushed to death, including a nine-year-old child.

"That was an accident," said Elek. "It wasn't my fault."

"Did I say it was? Yet it happened at a gathering of your followers. If the rally hadn't happened, no one would have died."

"*It wasn't my fault!*" Drops of spittle sprayed from Elek's lips.

She'd hit a nerve. She felt bad. Guilt over the deaths was a heavy burden to bear. She knew it too well. She bore some guilt herself. But she wanted to make Elek see sense.

"I didn't intend for anyone to get hurt," he went on. "I want to help people. But if some suffer so that—"

"Don't say it!"

"So that others benefit, perhaps that's a price worth paying."

"You said it." She glared at him. "I never had you down as the callous one. I always thought Arief took that crown."

"I am not callous. Only pragmatic." As he uttered the final two words, Elek turned away.

She waited, silent.

The busy chatter and movement in the cafe went on, heedless of the man and woman sitting at the window table not talking. If anyone thought about them at all, it was probably to surmise they were an odd couple. A young woman had taken a fancy to a big foreign man, but the relationship had turned sour, the cultural differences too great.

Eventually, Elek said, defeated, "All right. Things have been getting out of hand."

"So what are we going to do about it?"

"What will Arief allow us to do?"

"Why is any of this up to him? What were you saying about wanting everyone to be free agents, masters of their own destinies? What about us?"

"But Arief—"

"*Arief, Arief, Arief.* Screw Arief."

"If it wasn't for him I would be nobody. And you told me once he did something to you that helped you fight so well. We owe him. We can't just walk away."

"He gets more out of this than either of us. Seeing your influence over the crowds gives him a big kick. And those people who died?" Setia snapped her fingers. "*That* was how much he cared."

When Elek continued to look doubtful, she opened the

interface screen and turned it to face him. "These are the psychological and physical criteria for applying to be a colonist. We would have to pass the tests but I'm sure we can. It would be the perfect escape route. Don't you see? If we tried to walk away from all this Arief would come after us. He would talk us into coming back. You know how persuasive he is." It was more than that, but she didn't know how to put it into words. Once you were in Arief's presence it was nearly impossible to not do whatever he wanted.

She continued, "But if we leave aboard the *Bres* or another of Talman's ships, what could he do then? He wouldn't be able to get at us anymore. And you would have a shipload of people to talk to about your ideas. You never know, you might bring a different way of thinking and living to a new world and start a better version of human civilization. And I would help you. I believe in you, but the way things are going here is all wrong. It's turning ugly and I don't know how to stop it. Do you?"

Elek scanned the list on the screen but he didn't seem to be reading it. Setia could almost see the cogs of his mind whirring. She tensed, willing him to agree with her.

He murmured, "I don't know."

She exhaled her disappointment. "Would you think about it at least?"

"I guess it wouldn't hurt," he replied doubtfully.

"And don't mention a word of this to Arief. If he finds out, he'll do everything in his power to stop us. I guarantee it."

What a strange situation they were in. Arief had given them both what they wanted. Elek had gone from one of those dudes spouting his opinions on street corners, ignored by passersby, to a ground roots cultural phenomenon with hundreds of thousands of devotees. She was no longer a downtrodden street rat, living on the edge and clinging to survival. She had money, power, and respect. Yet it had all come with a price, unstated by the vendor at the time of the transaction.

In return for Arief's offering they had given over control of their lives. He had never stated it plainly but it was clear from his looks and attitude there was no going back for them, no matter who suffered or how many people died.

They were trapped.

"I know you!"

A skinny, middle-aged man in a checked shirt, dirty shorts, and blue plastic sandals was navigating the tables and customers to reach them. "I've been sitting there, thinking you looked familiar. It's Elek, right? I never expected to see you in a place like this. That's why it took me so long to recognize you."

Elek smiled his public smile, a mask Setia had seen him put on many times. "Please, join us." He pulled out the empty third seat at their table. "What's your name?"

28

____

For the first time since the announcement of the young Marine's suicide Yorkson had called everyone into the auditorium. On this occasion, the reason for the meeting was general knowledge: the *Defiant* had nearly reached her destination.

The atmosphere was predictably tense. The general chatter that usually accompanied large gatherings aboard ship was absent. Even the movements of the more than a hundred and fifty attendees were minimal. Quiet and stillness reigned in the packed room.

Patrin and Kayla sat on each side of Taylan and she held their hands. Wright had to be here too though she hadn't spotted him. He was on duty.

It was nearly crunch time. The results of the hard decision she'd made months ago were about to play out—for better or worse. Probably worse. But she'd done what she'd thought was right. There was no going back now.

"Mam," Kayla whispered, showing a rare moment of decorum, "you're hurting my hand."

"Sorry, sweetheart." Taylan slackened her grip.

Yorkson gave the command for the lighting to dim and it reduced to a minimal level. The shadowy heads and shoulders of the audience were barely visible.

The admiral gave another command, and a starscape brightened the center of the auditorium. Taylan counted five star systems circled by the radiant specks of their planets.

Yorkson cleared his throat. He'd moved out of the illumination of the stars and was entirely invisible, his voice disembodied. "Ladies and gentlemen, officers and Marines, thank you for coming. We are almost at the crucial part of our mission. I have called this briefing to update you on the latest information we have regarding our enemy. The skein mappers have narrowed down the source of the interference in Earth affairs to these five neighboring systems. At this time they're unable to provide us with more detailed intelligence. This is somewhat of a setback. The Alliance anticipated tackling the aliens on their home turf, in the same way they gatecrashed our system. We only have one ship. Should we visit all the systems? If so, in what order? Scan data is being assessed as I speak and we hope to glean facts to help inform our decision-making."

He went on, "However, an alternative interpretation is possible. The skein mappers speculate that the aliens may inhabit *all* the systems, that they represent a confederation. Perhaps, long ago, the species spread out to colonize nearby habitable planets, or perhaps life is abundant in this corner of the galaxy and we are dealing with not one but up to five intelligent life forms. It is a frustrating problem and—I make no bones about it—a dangerous one. The military among you know the wisdom of avoiding going in blind whenever possible. It seems in this case we might have to go in blind, deaf, and lacking most of our other senses too."

In response to murmurs of alarm he said, "I do not mean to scare you, only warn you. We don't know what to expect, and so when we do hopefully encounter these beings you must expect the unexpected."

A voice called out, "All I'm hearing is a lot of speculation. What's the plan?"

It was Meilyr. He and his brothers must have decided to lend their hands to the common cause after all.

Yorkson replied, "Good question. The plan will remain flexible as long as we have new data coming in. But, for now, it is to approach the nearest planet and attempt to make contact. Worlds in all five systems are habitable. We currently have no way of ascertaining which one harbors the aliens who visit Earth, if any."

"And what if we can't make contact?" This time Medwyn was the speaker. Taylan would recognize his gruff tones anywhere.

"Then we attempt to land the shuttle with a delegation aboard."

Medwyn asked sarcastically, "And I don't suppose one of the delegation is going to be you?"

"I will be in the party, yes."

This seemed to silence Medwyn. After a short pause, Meilyr said, "I would like to be aboard the vessel myself."

"You are most welcome, sir."

"How will you choose the other members of the delegation?" The question had come from Iolani.

"I think for everyone else it will be best to let the skein mappers advise us, but I am happy to listen to expressions of interest. For now, the choosing is somewhat premature. We have another week before we reach the nearest system, and then we must try to establish contact. This may take some time as there are many avenues to explore."

Medwyn growled, "If that Merlin fella wants to talk to us, he will."

"You may be correct," Yorkson agreed. "That's about all I have to tell you today. Questions?"

Taylan only half-listened to the inquiries and the admiral's responses. Her mind was on the delegation Yorkson had mentioned. She wasn't in any doubt she would be in it, and so would Wright and Arthur. If the skein mappers said Patrin and Kayla should go too, should she agree or say no? One thing putting her off allowing her kids to go to the alien planet wasn't the threat the hostile species posed, but other members of the visiting party. She was in no doubt Kala and Perran Orr would be chosen too, and she had no intention of allowing the pair anywhere near her offspring. Kala was as evil as Morgan and Merlin, if not more so.

"Taylan?"

She looked up. Abacha was standing in front of her. People were getting up from their seats. The meeting was over. Patrin and Kayla were on their way to the exit.

"How about a sparring session?" Abacha asked. "For old times' sake."

"Now?"

"It's as good a time as any, unless you have something else you need to do."

"No, I'm free. It's just..." She sought out her children again, but they'd left. "Sure. Let's do it now."

IN ALL THE ancient fighting arts practice sessions, somehow, she'd never worked with Abacha. It had always been Patrin or Arthur who had tutored or sparred with him.

As they stepped out into the gym in their protective gear, she said, "You know, I don't think we've done this since the *Valiant*."

"You could be right. It's been a long time. A lot's happened in between, for both of us, right?"

"You're not kidding."

"And now," he went on, "here we are again, back at the beginning."

She lightly punched his arm. "Don't get all philosophical on me, Abacha. That was never our style. What's it to be? How's your sword-fighting coming along?"

"Like I would be dumb enough to go up against you with a sword. I pick knives. That way, I'll stand a chance."

"Knives it is. It isn't going to make any difference, my friend."

They collected the blunt practice weapons and squared up. Taylan tossed her knife from one hand to the other. Abacha sighed and shook his head.

The gear they wore was wired to give audible signals when a blade made contact, and the number of sounds indicated the severity of the blow. A single tone meant a non-serious wound, right up to four tones in succession, which meant the receiver was immediately incapacitated and the blow was mortal without urgent medical attention.

Taylan leapt in and jabbed Abacha's shoulder. As she leapt out again a single tone sounded.

Abacha cursed. "Too damn light on your feet. Wait till I pin you down. You won't be so fast then."

She laughed.

He copied her maneuver. His words had been a bluff. But she jerked sideways in time to avoid the hit anyway, and dragged her knife across his ribs as he retreated.

Two tones sounded.

"Dammit," he muttered.

He didn't really mind. Abacha had always been good-humored about being beaten, unlike almost every other burly Royal Marine she'd fought.

So they continued, Taylan getting in minor but regular hits, Abacha trying the same but mostly failing. They could carry on like this for a long time, but eventually, Abacha's gear would sound the incapacitation tones anyway—in a real fight he would have suffered 'death by a thousand cuts'. But fighting like this was boring. It was time to end it.

She waited until the next time Abacha made his move, switched her knife to her other hand, took the hit to her arm, grabbed his neck and pulled him down with her free hand. Then she kneed him in the diaphragm, not too hard. Air exploded from his lungs. As he hovered, bent double, trying to breathe, she axe-kicked him between the shoulder blades. He toppled head-first to the deck.

She sat on his back, grasped his chin, and stretched out his neck. She didn't bother making the killing blow. "Concede?"

"Goddamn pain in the ass."

She chuckled and climbed off him. She didn't apologize. That would be condescending. "Another round?"

"Unless you mean beer," he replied, getting to his feet, "the answer's no."

"I'm fine with beer too."

As they walked to the showers, she said, "If it makes any difference, you should know the way I am is due to Merlin. If it wasn't for him you could probably beat me easily."

"What's that waste of space got to do with your fighting?"

"You're going to laugh, but..." Should she tell him she was descended from Lancelot? It was too outlandish. He would think she was crazy. "Merlin did something to my family. I suppose you could call it casting a spell on us. My fighting skills are in my bloodline. My dad was the same as me, and that's why Patrin's as good as he is."

"You mean it isn't because he's as big as a horse?"

"Ha, that too."

"How do you know? Did Merlin tell you?"

"Arthur did."

"I guess he would know." Abacha halted at the door to the men's showers. "So if it wasn't for Merlin, I would beat you at fighting *and* xiangqi."

She laughed. "That's moot."

He opened the door. "By the way, whatever happened to that old cat of yours?"

"Boots? He died last year."

"I'm sorry."

"Thanks. I was pretty cut up about it. Hey, Abacha, can I ask you a question?"

"Shoot."

"Are you an insomniac?"

He cocked an eyebrow. "Hell, no." Instantly, realization hit his features. He spluttered, "Uh, I mean, sometimes I have trouble..." His words petered out.

"Got you, you fibber."

"You did, but I lied for a good cause. When did you guess?"

"I'm not sure. Some time when I was out in the Australian outback, I think. Thanks for what you did for me back then. I appreciate it."

"No problem, little chick."

As Taylan showered, she recalled those late nights aboard the corvette HMSS *Daisy*, when the two of them had whiled away the hours playing xiangqi. He'd pretended he also couldn't sleep so he could be a friend to someone he sensed was in pain.

Little chick.

He knew she hated it when he called her that.

She smiled.

29

The sparring session in the gym with Abacha felt like a watershed moment. As Taylan curled up next to Wright that night, it came to her that her old friend had asked to fight, to reconnect, because it might be their last chance. In a few days they would be facing the aliens interfering in Earth affairs, and no one had the slightest idea what might happen.

It was a time for just-in-case goodbyes, final words, a time to make peace and ask forgiveness.

The following morning, she went to see Meilyr and his brothers. The last time she'd done this the reception she'd received hadn't exactly been welcoming. Taking a deep breath, she pressed the door chime.

"Taylan," Meilyr said gravely in greeting. He was sitting down, pulling on a sock. Madog and Medwyn seemed to be waiting for him.

"Ugh, bad news is back again," Medwyn spat. "What is it this time? The Alliance is planning on putting everyone from West BI out the airlock? Kala Orr is going to bunk in our cabin?"

"I don't know how you can blame me for telling you the truth," Taylan complained. "Unless you'd rather I kept what I knew a secret?"

"No," said Meilyr. "He doesn't mean that. Do you, Medwyn?"

The brother softly growled a reply but she couldn't make it out.

Addressing her, Meilyr said, "Come in. Don't stand in the doorway like an idiot." When she stepped into the cabin he went on, "We're grateful to you for letting us know the truth. Yorkson is still denying it, but I know who I believe."

"What are you going to do?" she asked. "Are you going to sit out the mission like you said?"

"We haven't—"

At the same time, Medwyn replied, "Yes!"

Meilyr finished, "Come to a decision."

"*I'm* not helping them," said Medwyn, "whatever you might say, brother."

"And that's your choice, but this family has acted as one all our lives. That was how Mam, bless her soul, brought us up—to support each other. There's strength in numbers, she always said."

"Wrong," said Medwyn. "That was how we acted all our lives until *she* turned up." Even if he hadn't given Taylan a narrowed glance, it was clear to all present who he meant.

In the awkward pause that followed, Taylan said, "About that..."

"Yes?" asked Madog, hands on hips. It was a challenge.

She swallowed. She hadn't prepared what she wanted to say, and now, with all three brothers watching her expectantly, her mind was suddenly blank.

The door slid open and Marc walked in.

She groaned. It was exactly the wrong timing. If they began a discussion on what had happened on Ynys Môn with Marc around he would defend her, which would spark Medwyn to attack, and then there would be a big argument.

"Taylan," Marc said, "nice to see...What are you doing?"

She was pushing him by his chest out of the cabin. "Could you wait outside for a bit?"

"Uh, okay." The closing door cut off the view of his surprised expression.

She turned to face the three men. They, of all the West BI Resistance, had done so much to help her. They had literally saved her life. Perhaps it would be best to start with that. "First of all, thanks for coming to Patrin's party. I appreciate the gesture. It meant a lot. But I think there's more to be said before we can mend our bridges." She paused before going on, "I also want to thank you for all you did for me. You gave me supplies and equipment to use when I was trying to find my kids—supplies and equipment you could scarce afford to give. When I got shot, you nursed me back to health. If it wasn't for you guys, I would never have made it to Australia and my kids would be dead. There's no price I can pay, nothing I can give, that's sufficient payment for everything you did."

"Oh, you paid us back all right," Medwyn commented wryly.

She ignored him. "I never intended, that night on Ynys Môn, for Marc to help me. He guessed what I was doing and he wanted to come along. I tried to stop him but he wouldn't have it. In the end, I did let him help. That's on me. Maybe I should have argued harder and he would have listened eventually. Then he wouldn't have been hurt."

Somewhere in the three men's frowns, she saw the pain of seeing their brother badly burned, the sense of betrayal from her after everything they'd done, and the disgust that she'd sided with Crusaders over her own people. She didn't know how to make that look go away. Perhaps it never would. Perhaps the subject would always be sore. It was time to put it to bed once and for all.

"But I didn't argue," she said. "I accepted that Marc was doing what he wanted to do. He'd weighed up the facts and come to his own decision, and I respected that. He was acting of his own free will. He suffered terrible consequences, but that's on him, not me."

It was harsh but true. The men's frowns hardened, but she wasn't going to back down now. She'd hit on the heart of their disagreement. "You all see Marc as your baby brother, someone to protect. But even all those years ago at Ynys Môn he was already a grown man. He'd been big enough and strong enough to carry me all the way back to your hideout, remember? How old was he? Twenty-one? Twenty-two? My point is, he had a right to decide for himself. The exact same right you were complaining the Alliance took from you when it lied to you."

The men gave no reply. Even Medwyn had nothing to say for once.

She continued, "You're never going to agree with me about what Marc and I did. I wanted to protect the Crusaders' innocent children. You saw any harm that came to them as unfortunate collateral damage. You weighed their hurt against the hurt our kids had suffered. I couldn't think like that and I never will. But when it comes to Marc, I'm asking you to let this go and stop blaming me."

Medwyn said, "We came to your stupid party and my brothers are speaking to you again, stars help them. Why isn't that enough for you? What do you care how we feel about what you did to Marc?"

"Because if you can forgive and forget then maybe I can too."

"Forgive *us*?!" Medwyn spluttered.

"Forgive myself."

Despite all she'd said about Marc's right to choose what he

did, his body-encompassing burns from the incendiary device, the clinging oil continuing to melt his skin, remained an image seared into her mind and heart. If she knew his siblings didn't believe his injuries had been her fault that could help stop it haunting her.

Seconds of silence ticked past.

Then Meilyr got up from his bunk and crossed the cabin to her side. The big man enveloped her in his arms and she sank into his chest. He didn't say anything but it didn't matter. Nothing needed to be said. When he released her, she caught Madog's gaze. He gave a small nod. Medwyn was looking down, refusing to go along with his brothers' change of heart.

Oh, well. Two out of three isn't bad.

The door opened.

Marc said, "I've been out here five minutes. Can I come in now?"

Seren had arrived and was waiting with him.

Taylan noticed something about her she realized she should have noticed a long time ago. There was no mistaking the bump that rounded out her belly. "Seren, I didn't know you were pregnant!"

She smiled and stepped into the cabin with Marc. "We only found out after we left Mars. I've been trying to disguise it for months."

"But there's no disguising it now," said Marc proudly.

"You've been getting medical care?" asked Taylan gently.

The news was not as joyful as it would have been on Earth. Pregnancy wasn't technically 'allowed' in space. As well as space travel being inherently dangerous, there were known risks to the fetus from radiation. The medical staff aboard would have strongly advised termination.

"Yes, the doctor's been great," Seren replied. She added, her eyes shining, "I couldn't get rid of it. I just couldn't."

"I understand," Taylan said. "It's a shame you didn't tell me earlier. I've been through it twice myself. I could have helped you."

"I didn't want anyone to know," Seren explained. "I didn't want to be judged. But now the cat's out of the bag anyway, I might take you up on that."

Taylan said goodbye to the family and returned to her cabin, where Wright was only just awake. He opened his eyes sleepily. "Where have you been?"

"I went to see the brothers from West BI."

His eyes snapped wide and he shot to a sitting position. "Stars, Taylan. What did you tell them this time?"

"Don't worry," she replied, climbing onto the bed. She lay down next to him. "It was something between me and them. We're good now."

30

"I thought you might be one of the chosen few," Wright said as Iolani joined the group waiting in the shuttle bay.

"You did?" she replied, adjusting her stance awkwardly. "I never knew body armor was so uncomfortable. You're better at this than me. I thought I was only here as a consultant or maybe to create the Habitat. I've never met these aliens you call Merlin and Morgan."

"You're our resident expert on living organisms. You gave some interesting insights while we were on the *Dauntless*. I thought what you said about the alien species being very long-lived made a lot of sense."

"Huh, not that anyone took any notice of me."

"They're taking notice now. The skein mappers have spoken."

The space was beginning to fill up. The final list of names for the delegation had gone out at breakfast and now everyone was arriving.

Taylan looked like she was having the worst day of her life. She was pale and haggard and her shoulders drooped. But he couldn't say or do anything to help her. Patrin and Kayla's names had been on the list and they would be going to the planet with her and the rest of the team. Even the presence of her friends from the Resistance days wasn't cheering her up. She'd barely raised a wan smile when they'd entered the bay.

Arthur was here, naturally, along with Colbourn, Abacha, Kevin, and Ford. Yorkson's name hadn't been flagged by the mappers, which was probably just as well. The *Defiant* needed her admiral. If something bad happened and none of the delegation made it back to the ship she needed someone to get everyone else home.

Some Marines who weren't on the list would be coming along too, seasoned troops for backup in case of conflict. No one had any idea whether that was likely or the aliens had another plan in store. They had to know humans had come all the way from Earth to find them. What they would do about it was anyone's guess.

Their planet—assuming it *was* their planet—showed no sign of organic life though it was capable of supporting it. The gravity and atmosphere were so similar to Earth's there was no particular need for the delegation to wear armored EVA suits, though they were wearing them nevertheless as a precaution. Yorkson had picked a landmass near the equator at random as the landing site. The ship's scanners hadn't picked up any signs of artificial constructions where the aliens might live or work.

It was baffling but they had no choice except to attempt to make contact.

Yorkson walked into the bay. "Good morning, everyone. I've come to wish you bon voyage and good luck. If I could give you some final advice I would, but unfortunately this is a situation that's new to all of us and we must play it by ear. We will be in constant comm contact for the duration of your trip and while you're on the surface. Brigadier Colbourn is to be your commanding officer, for military and civilians alike, so please be sure to follow her orders to the letter."

Taylan will be overjoyed.

But when Wright looked for her reaction, she didn't appear to have even heard what Yorkson said.

Two more figures appeared, accompanied by guards. Kala Orr and her son had arrived. A palpable shiver ran through the group and an icy pall fell on the general atmosphere. Orr and her offspring stood some distance away, but the change in their appearance since the beginning of the voyage was noticeable. Both looked unhealthy from their long incarceration. Hollowed shadows surrounded their eyes and their cheekbones stuck out.

"That's it," said the admiral. "Time to board."

He stood at the ramp, shook the hand of each civilian as they passed him, and returned the Marines' salutes. Wright was reminded of Hans Jonte doing something similar when they'd boarded the shuttle that would take them to the *Defiant*. Only no media reps were here to watch and report. This was not for show.

As they took their seats, Taylan asked him, "What are you going to be on this mission?"

"What do you mean?"

"Are you my husband and stepfather to my kids, or are you Lieutenant-Colonel Wright, Royal Marine?"

"Can't I be both?"

"Can you? If it comes down to it and you have to choose between your family and your duty, which will you pick?"

"I can't see how that'll be a choice I have to make."

The look she gave him cut to his soul.

He took her hand. "You, Patrin, and Kayla come first."

THE SURFACE of the alien planet was a dry, dusty place. A black plain stretched out to distant, bare hills, under a pale orange sky. The black dust hung in the air, creating a haze that faintly obscured the dismal view.

"We are the first human beings to set foot on an exoplanet," announced Colbourn. "We have beaten Ua Talman's colonization project. Drink in the experience, ladies and gentlemen, for no one else will be able to say they've done the same."

The brigadier was waxing unusually eloquent but Wright felt a sense of anti-climax. There was nothing here. No Merlin, Morgan, or any other aliens, not even any living organisms as far as he could tell. If it weren't for the different coloring and Earth-like gravity and atmosphere, they could be back on Mars.

"This is it?" asked Kevin. "I've seen more life in the outback. The skein mappers must have it wrong. Nothing's ever lived here."

"I don't get it," said Iolani. She was squatting down, running a handful of soil through her fingers. "In these conditions I would expect this area to be teeming with life. I would need to look at this stuff under a microscope, but it appears entirely barren." She stood up. "We know from Ua Talman's probes that living organisms exist on other worlds, even if they aren't intelligent. Life isn't *that* rare."

"So why aren't we seeing it?" Colbourn asked.

"I'm sorry. I have no idea."

"Is it possible it died out?"

"Species go extinct all the time, but a planetary wide wipe-out? Extremely unlikely. Once life appears it usually becomes self-sustaining. It's very difficult to eradicate. An event of the magnitude to sterilize an entire planet would leave signs—background radiation, evidence of a massive impact. *Something.* I've examined the scan data. There's nothing like that here. No reason for the lack of life. I found it hard to believe until now."

Colbourn asked, "Could we simply be unlucky, and we happen to have landed in a particularly lifeless area? Should we try somewhere else?"

"With respect," said Meilyr, "this isn't an exploratory expedition. We aren't planning on colonizing the place. We're here to find the aliens that have been interfering in our affairs. Where are they? If they're as all-seeing as everyone makes out, they must know we're here. Rather than flying off somewhere else, shouldn't we stick around and wait for them to come to us?"

"We could be waiting a long time," said Wright. "I've a feeling that if they really wanted to speak to us they would be here already."

Arthur chipped in, "Merlin would not waste any time if he wanted to meet us. Either he is not here or he does not wish to grant us an audience."

"My money is on the latter," Taylan muttered.

"Maybe they're still deciding what to do about us," said Kevin. "If you're a bully and your victim turns up on your doorstep, what *do* you do?"

"*I* would not hesitate," said a deep, female voice. "I would squash them flat."

It was the first time Kala Orr had spoken so far. During all of the trip down to the surface, putting on their EVA suits, walking out and seeing the planet, neither she nor her son had said a word.

And now she had said something, her tone sent a shiver down Wright's spine. There was a creepy edge to it, a note of madness.

Colbourn walked away from the group, out over the dusty ground. The soil was so fine and dry, it lifted in soft puffs at each of her footsteps. Everyone watched her in silence. A wind swept over the plain, raising a black cloud. The brigadier covered about fifty meters before turning and walking back. Perhaps she was in a one-to-one with Yorkson.

She reached them.

"We wait."

31

Elek was fast becoming a global phenomenon. Setia hadn't been able to help but watch with a mixture of pride and fear as his followers grew into their millions. It had taken years for the word-of-mouth movement to take hold, but once people joined they stayed. This was not a flash-in-the-pan thing, a viral media takeover, here one day and gone the next. It was a long-lasting, vital doctrine.

Elek would not have called it that. He would have called it a philosophy, a way of thinking, not a belief system. But his people carried a fervor that was plain to anyone with eyes to see. It was like the old Crusader cult, though dressed up more nicely with clever words and phrases like self-determination, development of the individual spirit, and personal sovereignty. The result was the same. Elek was worshipped.

And he kind of liked it.

That was what disappointed Setia. She'd known him a long time, from the earliest days in downtown Spiral City. They'd been similar then. Like her, he'd come from a rough back-ground, owning little more than the clothes on his back. Consequently, also like her, he'd been humble, grateful simply for a full stomach and a day that passed without trouble. The only difference between them had been his desire to improve the lot of the lowest in society. She, on the other hand, had believed it was up to every man and woman to improve their own lot if they so chose, and that avoiding people like Pratam was probably a good first step. She still believed that. As to what Elek truly believed now, she wasn't sure anymore. He'd changed.

She'd given him a chance to get out a few months ago and he hadn't taken it. Her perspective on her friend had altered that day. It had been like she was seeing the new Elek for the first time. She didn't like what she saw.

"Setia, are you ready?" Arief had opened the door to her room.

She was surprised he'd come himself. The movement had any number of members willing to be unpaid servants and perform menial tasks like reminding Elek's right-hand woman of her duties. Not only were the workers unpaid, they often donated their own money for the privilege.

"Yes," she replied dully. "I'll be there in a minute."

"Don't be late. This event is more important than most." He left.

He'd been referring to the fact that Hans Jonte, former Prime Minister of the Britannic Isles, would be attending. Jonte lending his face to Elek's campaign would carry a lot of weight even though he was now a has-been. She wasn't sure if that was the ex-PM's intention or if he was only curious and wanted to see the man behind all the chatter.

Nowadays, Elek had a retinue of bodyguards. Her services were no longer required, but for some reason it pleased Arief to see her still performing her role, albeit in a symbolic capacity. Whenever she stood at the leader's side, dressed in her uniform, it would bring a sly smile to his face. She'd never figured out what it was about.

Why wouldn't he accept her resignation? What did it matter to him whether she left or stayed? Did it have something to do with what he'd done to her in that alley when she'd faced Soleh? She would gladly let him take back her strange abilities but maybe he couldn't. Knowing Arief, it was more likely he wouldn't.

Sighing, she got to her feet.

~

THE STADIUM WAS PACKED. By all accounts, it was the largest crowd Elek had ever gathered. Bright in the spotlights, he stood before a sea of faces covering all available space. Setia couldn't imagine what it must be like to stand in the audience, people pressing in on every side, but no one seemed bothered. Every face shone with excitement. Such was the devotion Elek inspired.

She took up her position near the edge of the stage, ready to repel over-excited fans who decided to try to get up close and personal with their idol.

Elek began to speak, and the buzz of the watchers instantly faded to silence. Setia shifted her weight from one foot to the other. She'd heard him say roughly the same things for years, sometimes varying a theme or telling a new story, but it was always the identical messages. He couldn't be blamed for that, but she was heartily tired of listening to him.

Arief stood in the wings on the opposite side of the stage, looking beyond Elek into the crowd. Even at the distance, Setia could make out his dark eyes moving hungrily, as if eating the adulation. She wanted to vomit. But she was stuck for another couple of hours at least. To distract herself she allowed her mind to wander back to her youth. She recalled Aulia, a good friend. What had happened to her? What were things like in

Spiral City now? Was Pratam still plying his trade or had the authorities caught up with him?

Distant voices dragged her back to the present. On the far side of the stadium, opposite where Elek stood, a dispute had started up. The shouts were too far away to make out what was being said. Heads in the audience turned however. Elek paused. Others could be heard now, telling the arguers to shut up.

"Be ready," said a voice in Setia's ear. It was Arief speaking through her comm.

"Ready for what?" she asked. "What's going on?"

"It has begun," was all Arief would say.

She comm'd the in-crowd security for information on the situation, but her operatives happened to be far from the disturbance and people were crammed in so tightly they could only move slowly toward it.

Then the screaming started.

In the half-light hanging over the stadium, pulse fire flashed out. The shots seemed to be coming from the same place as the arguing voices.

Setia cursed and yelled into her mic. The operatives in the audience had to get to the shooters now. At the same time, she rushed onto the stage. Elek was standing there like a dumbass, transfixed by the mass-shooting taking place before his eyes.

"Get down," she shouted, pulling him to the floor. "It's you they really want."

Keeping him low, she pushed him to the side of the stage.

"But why?" he asked incredulously as he crawled along. "Why would anyone do this?"

"Because people are crazy. What do you think I've been doing all this time? There are always maniacs out to get you. They've just upped their game."

They'd reached the wings. She pushed him out of sight. He

was safe for the moment, but she needed to get him to an armored car and away from this place.

As she put in the call, she spotted Arief. He remained in the same area he'd stood all along, gazing out over the crowd. The pleasure written on his features was sickening.

32

———

Patrin leaned apathetically on the shuttle's hull, his gaze running along the horizon. The wind was whipping up black dust devils in the deep orange dusk. Hours had passed and there was no sign of the aliens. How much longer would they have to wait? Almost everyone had gone into the shuttle to sit down. Maybe he should do that too, but the prospect seemed even more boring than waiting outside.

A large figure loomed in the corner of his vision. No one else matched his height. "Arthur. I thought you'd gone inside with the others."

"I had, but I came out again. You and I never seem to have an opportunity to speak alone with each other, not since the days of your riding lessons."

"You're right." When he thought about it, Patrin suspected Mam of keeping him away from the king. "I miss those lessons. They were great—until the last one." Was that why his mother had gone to lengths to ensure he and Arthur were never alone together? He'd never told her about the assassination attempt but she could have found out about it another way.

"I enjoyed them too, even though the final one was eventful.

Patrin, now I have you alone, I would like to tell you something." The king's tone was serious.

Patrin looked around. Only the Marines remained outside the shuttle, guarding it in case the aliens decided to put in an appearance. "What is it?"

"I have a strong foreboding something bad is going to happen. I knew Merlin most of my life, and though I never guessed he was not from Earth, I believe I grew to know him well. He will not take this visit favorably. He enjoys having human beings under his control, and by coming here we're challenging his power. He won't like it and he will seek to punish us. The same applies to Morgan, only more so. She is truly evil. You can see it in Kala Orr and Perran. Morgan's poison runs like quicksilver in their veins."

"That's what you wanted to tell me?" Patrin asked. "I appreciate it, but I don't think that's news to anyone."

"That is not all." Arthur placed a hand on Patrin's shoulder. "My boy, though you are not of my blood you are like a son to me, the son I would have preferred over the one I was given."

Patrin was touched. "That's a great honor, sir."

Arthur continued, "The foreboding I feel extends doubly to you. I don't know if it's due to my affection for you or because the story of my life is playing out again. Many events that have occurred since I was woken from my long sleep have felt like that to me." He leaned close until their helmets were nearly touching. "There may come a time very soon when the opportunity arises to risk your life on my behalf. I am asking you now, do not do it."

"I don't think that's likely. Mam won't allow me anywhere near any action. That's what the Royal Ma—"

"No one knows what the next few hours or days hold. No one. My heart tells me we are moving toward a cataclysm from which few will escape. I hope with all my being you are one of them. I ask you again, do not risk yourself for my benefit. My life has been rich and long. If the end comes soon, I shall not rue it. Do you understand?"

"I understand, sir."

The king squeezed his shoulder and then walked away.

A fizz of excitement had replaced Patrin's boredom, though he had no idea what half of the conversation had been about. He supposed he'd meant it when he'd agreed to not do anything dangerous to save Arthur, but he still strongly doubted the situation would even come up. Mam was like one of Carys's hawks when it came to protecting him. She would whisk Kayla and him as far away from any trouble as she could at the first sign of it.

"Patrin?"

Kayla had arrived.

"Mam says you have to come inside. You can't stay out here without her. It isn't safe."

"I thought she might say that. Why didn't she comm me?"

"She has been comming you. Are you coming in?"

He realized he'd closed other channels for his one-to-one with Arthur and hadn't noticed the bleeps.

"Yes, I'm coming."

As they walked to the ramp, Kayla said, "I'm really sorry about my speech at your birthday party."

"Why? I thought it was sweet."

"I mean the bit about you never having a girlfriend. I shouldn't have said that. I don't know why it popped out. I'm always saying the wrong thing."

"It's okay, sis. I know you don't mean to do it."

They passed through the airlock and into the passenger cabin, where the sound of chatter was loud. Kala Orr and Perran were the only people who were silent, sitting at the back, handcuffed to their armrests. The other passengers were sitting in groups. Mam was deep in conversation with the men from West BI. TJ was sitting with them too, though he wasn't speaking. He looked as bored as Patrin had felt a few minutes ago.

It only took a moment for Patrin to realize why.

He strode down the aisle to the huddle.

"You're back at last," his mother said. "Don't go out there by yourself again, okay?"

"I won't. Mam, don't you think it would be more polite to speak English around TJ? He can't understand a word you're all saying."

"Oh, shit." She grasped TJ's forearm, saying, "Sorry." Turning to the men, she said, "English, guys, English."

They also apologized in the main language of the Britannic Isles.

But before they could continue their conversation, Brigadier Colbourn stood up at the front of the cabin. "Orders have arrived to return to the *Defiant*. Please prepare for takeoff."

"What's happening?" asked Meilyr. "Are we coming back here later or trying something else?"

"We will try another planet," Colbourn replied.

Patrin sat down and fastened his safety belt. He couldn't see much point in attempting to make contact in another of the star systems the skein mappers had identified. From all he'd heard about the aliens, if they wanted to speak to them they would. The experience here seemed to say that wasn't going to happen.

Maybe Arthur had got it wrong.

THE SHUTTLE DEPARTED the site of humanity's first encounter with an exoplanet, into a darkening sky. Their attempt to challenge the aliens interfering in Earth's affairs had come and gone without any kind of a result.

"I hope they're all like this," Taylan said.

"All the planets we visit?" Wright asked.

"Every single one. I hope they're all dreary and boring and lifeless, and we can pack up and go home. We can tell the skein mappers they're on something and they need a serious re-think."

"I suppose it is possible they got it all wrong. The scientists only have the files they were sent from the *Dauntless*. No explanations or feedback on their interpretation of the information. I don't know enough about it to even guess."

"Me neither," said Taylan. "It doesn't stop me hoping. I'm really sorry about excluding you from the conversation back there, by the way. I wasn't thinking."

"To be honest it's quite flattering. You all seemed to think of me as one of the group and so I should naturally speak your language. And I like listening to it, even though I don't understand a word. Do you remember on the *Valiant* when I assumed you and Arthur could understand each other?"

"Ha! Yeah, I do. I haven't heard him speak his native tongue for a long time, but from memory it did sound familiar, just not comprehensible."

"That was ignorant of me."

"No, it was an easy mistake to make. After all, he is from the same place, only not the same time. You weren't to know, and you were kind and compassionate in the way you treated him, even when he was out of control. That was one of the first things I liked about you." She rested her head on his shoulder.

The scene outside the window was fading to black and stars were winking to life.

A streak of light flew past.

"What was that?" she asked, sitting up.

Others in the cabin had seen it too. People craned their necks to see out the windows.

A second streak cut across the blackness, brighter than the first. The light briefly illuminated the cabin.

Alarmed voices rose. At the back, the Marines began to put on their helmets. A second later, Colbourn's command arrived over the intercom: civilians had to do the same. "Please check your safety belts are securely fastened," she added.

"What does it mean?" Taylan asked.

"I think we're under attack," Wright replied before lowering his helmet over his head. The next time he spoke it was via comm. "Taylan, I need to help Colbourn with this."

"You *said* me and the kids come first."

"Don't worry, I won't forget about you." He got out of his seat and ran down the aisle. Before he'd reached the brigadier, another flash of light exploded. The cabin turned dark and the shuttle dipped.

"Mam?" Kayla asked. She and Patrin were sitting across the aisle. "What's going on?"

"I've a feeling the aliens decided to pay us a visit after all. There's no need to worry. We'll be all right. We just need to make it back to the *Defiant*." In truth, she was very worried. If the aliens were attacking them as Wright guessed, they were in extreme danger in the shuttle. It was armored and carried defensive weaponry but it was no match for a military starship, especially not the kind Merlin and Morgan's species could build.

About a minute passed with no more light streaks. Wright was in consultation with Colbourn and the Marines had readied their arms. The civilians were simply confused. No one had told them anything since the command to put on their helmets.

Surely they must be nearly at the *Defiant*? The trip to the surface had taken less than an hour, and it must have been at least forty-five minutes since they'd taken off.

Several Marines left their seats and stood in the aisle, lined up facing the airlock. Wright crossed the cabin to join them. He and Colbourn seemed to expect the aliens to try to board.

Taylan leaned out from her seat and looked back, making eye contact with Arthur. She opened a comm. "Do you know what's going on?"

He shook his head. "TJ told me to stay in my seat. But when the *Dauntless* was attacked, the Merlins and Morgans came through the airlock. That must be what they think might happen here."

"The Merlins and Morgans, plural?"

"There were many of them, all the same. They were carrying pulse rifles the same as the ones the Royal Marines use."

Shit.

She switched her comm to speak to Patrin and Kayla. "If the airlock is breached, get down as low as you can and don't lift your heads until I or TJ tell you."

"Is someone going to try to board us?" Patrin asked.

"Maybe. I don't know. Just remember what I said."

None of it made any sense. The aliens had to have the technological capability to vaporize the shuttle, and the *Defiant* for that matter. If they'd developed the ability to transform into galaxy-faring clouds, to move starships vast distances, to live thousands of years, they were vastly more advanced than humans. What were they playing at?

Maybe that was it. They were playing. They were having fun at their visitors' expense, showing them who was boss.

A light so bright it blinded her flamed out. Simultaneously, a crackling hiss burst over Taylan's comm. The shuttle veered right so hard she was slammed to the left. "Hold on!" she yelled to her kids. "Hold onto something. Anything. And don't let go!"

An ear-splitting crack resounded through the cabin. It was as she'd predicted—the shuttle's hull had been breached. The split was out of sight somewhere up ahead, but its general position was clear from the way everything loose flew toward it. The

Marines in the aisle battled against the escaping atmosphere and flying objects to return to their seats.

"Taylan, are you okay?" It was Wright. "You and the kids are strapped in, right?"

"We're fine."

Patrin and Kayla had hunched over and were holding onto their armrests like life itself.

"Where are you?" she asked. "Are you in a seat?"

She could no longer distinguish him from the other Marines in their identical EVA suits.

"Working on it. We're nearly home. The pilot says another two minutes."

Two minutes was a long time when you were under attack, and a long distance in space travel terms. Another hit like that and they wouldn't make it.

"Wright, come back. There's nothing else you can do now."

"I'll try."

She leaned out again, trying to spot him. Most of the Marines had made it back to their seats.

There he is!

One Marine detached from the rest. His body bent against the force of depressurization, gripping seat backs, he slowly made his way up the aisle. When he reached their seats she grabbed him and held onto him until his safety belt was fastened.

The blinding light flashed again, and suddenly the rush of escaping air was silent. Taylan could hear nothing at all via external comm. Confused, she looked up and then down the cabin.

As her gaze traveled to the rear, her heart stopped.

The tail section was *gone*.

At the end of the aisle was nothing but empty space. The final rows of Marines had been lost, either killed in the blast or tossed into the vacuum. This close to the planet they would be drawn in by its gravity and plummet to the surface.

"Holy shit," Wright breathed. The place where he'd been standing a moment before had vanished.

"The engines are on the wings, aren't they?" asked Taylan.

"Uh huh. We still have a chance." He began to get up. "I need to—"

"No, stay here. What can you realistically do?"

His shoulders slumped. "You're right. Those men and women though..."

"Where's Colbourn?"

"She survived, but only just. Her row's now the last one."

Taylan looked back again. There was nothing any of the people nearest the hole could do except hope the shuttle held together.

"We're here," said Wright.

The starship up ahead was a welcome sight, the opening to her landing bay even better to see. The shuttle flew in and bumped down like a fledgling on its first flight, leaving the cabin hanging at a crazy angle.

But they were back. They'd made it.

How long the respite would last was anyone's guess.

33

"Patrin, Kayla, go to Patrin's cabin and lock the door." Taylan gave each of them a pulse rifle she'd taken from the shuttle's store. She'd also taken one for herself. "Don't take off your armor, and if anyone tries to break in, use these. You know how. Don't hesitate to shoot, and don't come out until I, TJ, or someone you trust tells you it's safe." Swallowing the lump in her throat, she took a close look at her kids, praying it wasn't for the last time.

"What are you going to do, Mam?" Kayla asked tremulously.

"If the aliens attack I'm going to help defend the ship."

"Can't you stay with us?"

"I can't, sweetheart. I'm sorry. They're going to need everyone they can get, especially since losing those poor men and women on the shuttle."

"I want to fight too," said Patrin.

"No, you're too young."

"But I—"

"This isn't a discussion!" Softening her tone, she explained, "I need you to look after Kayla, like you did before, okay? I need you to do it for my peace of mind. And you're not trained to fight like a Marine. I am." She hugged them both. "Do what I say now. Please."

Patrin and Kayla obediently left. She watched them go, a gash ripping through her heart. She was suddenly home in West BI, thrusting a screaming Kayla into the arms of an old woman, asking her to look after her children. Was she making the same mistake again? Would it be better to keep them by her side?

"Taylan."

Wright was running toward her.

"What's happening?" she asked. Everything had been in turmoil since the shuttle landed. The survivors from the trip to the alien planet had scrambled to get out of the destroyed vessel, and personnel on the *Defiant* were racing to and fro as alarms sounded.

"We're at battle stations," Wright replied. "We're leaving the system, returning to Earth."

It was obvious why. The aliens' act of aggression had made it clear there would be no meetings, no discussion of their activities on Earth, no attempt to come to a resolution. Humans were not welcome on their patch.

"Any signs of their ships?" she asked.

"Nothing yet. The scanners couldn't even detect the ship that attacked the shuttle. The data say there's nothing in the direction where the pulse bolts originated. On the *Dauntless...* Wait." He seemed to register her rifle. "You're going to help?"

"Of course. Where do I go?"

"Thanks. I was hoping you would. That thing about putting you and the kids first..."

"It doesn't mean I don't fight. Just, if it comes down to it, please do all you can to save Patrin and Kayla, even if it means neglecting your duties."

"I... Okay, it's a deal. Stick with me. We're going to airlock

A." They set off at a run. "When the aliens attacked the *Dauntless*—"

"Arthur told me. A horde of Merlins and Morgans?"

"It was surreal. But Iolani figured out a way to defeat them. We can do it again if they pull the same trick."

Taylan doubted they would. If their tactic didn't succeed last time, why would they try it again? "Let's hope the attack on the shuttle was a shot across the bows and they'll leave us alone when they see we're leaving."

"I hope so too."

The alternative didn't bear contemplating. Pulse bolts from an invisible ship? And it had to be a particle beam that had cut off the shuttle's tail section. The *Defiant* carried the latest weaponry but it was useless if they had nothing to aim at.

By the time she and Wright reached the airlock, twenty or so Marines were already waiting for his arrival. Arthur was here too. He'd brought Excalibur and he'd taken off his helmet.

When Wright challenged him about it, he replied, "I do not like to wear it and I had no need of it last time, my friend. What makes you think I'll need it now?"

"Your sword was useless last time too," Wright countered. "Maybe you would be better off with a rifle?"

"If Merlin allows me to fight, he will, regardless of my weapon. The decision is in his hands."

"What's *that* about?" Taylan asked Wright. "Does it mean I shouldn't look forward to Arthur slicing off Merlin's head?"

"Oh, he'll do it. It just won't have any effect. Get ready. You're at the rear."

"But—"

"That's an order."

She clenched her jaw. "Yes, *sir*."

She stood next to the Marine farthest from the airlock. Despite the inertia dampeners, the acceleration force of the

Defiant's rapid departure dragged at her. She activated the magnetic soles of her boots.

WRIGHT HATED INCLUDING Taylan in the fight but he had no choice. They needed her. Rejecting the support of a skilled fighter in this situation was madness, even if she was his wife.

"SITREP, Lieutenant-Colonel."

Colbourn must have made it to the bridge.

"In position at airlock A, Brigadier."

"And the rest of the airlocks?"

"All covered."

As before on the *Dauntless*, he was responsible for repelling boarders.

"Any sign of anything, Brigadier?"

"Not a thing. We didn't see it, but the *Defiant* was firing in defense of the shuttle. Unfortunately, our computer can't extrapolate the coordinates of the hostile ship fast enough to hit her when firing back. I'll keep you posted." She cut the comm.

Wright waited for the judder of the aliens' ship securing a hold on theirs. But nothing happened. Seconds turned into minutes. He forced himself to breathe and ease his racing pulse. Things had been bad on the *Dauntless* but at least Taylan and her kids had been safe on Earth. He regretted persuading her to join the mission. Would she forgive him? He hoped she had the chance.

Arthur stood still as a statue, Excalibur balanced in two hands, and the Marines were ready.

Surely if the aliens were going to attack they would have done so by now. Their ship had been right there in the vicinity. All she had to do was turn her firepower on the *Defiant*. There was no way the enemy feared a reprisal. It had everything on its side.

Perhaps they were going to let the humans go.

Wright checked his HUD. Eleven minutes had passed since Colbourn's comm. They would be nearing the edge of the planetary system.

How long would Yorkson wait before giving the All Clear?

If only they could get away, albeit with their fingers burned. The return journey would be more joyful than boring, and when they got home they could tackle the aliens' interference there.

He tensed.

Something had changed.

He could not say what. Perhaps there had been a tiny check in the ship's movement or an alteration in its electrical field, but something had happened.

"We're under attack," came Colbourn's comm. "Pulse cannon. At the ready, Wright."

He relayed the alert to his team and the teams at every airlock.

There was nothing to do now but wait. Either the aliens would try to board, possibly after disabling the *Defiant*, or they wouldn't. If their intention was to destroy the human's ship, there wasn't anything he could do about it. The work was down to Yorkson and the weapons officers on the bridge.

Taylan hailed him in a one-to-one comm.

"Yes?" he answered, his tone automatically softening.

"I-I—"

"I love you too."

He couldn't imagine what she was going through. The thought of losing her was agony, but she was contemplating the deaths of her children, a torment she'd already suffered once in her life. And here he was, putting her through it again. He contemplated apologizing but how would that help?

"Taylan, if you want to be with Patrin and Kayla…"

"No, I'll stay here for now. Until I know for sure there's no hope."

"TJ?" Arthur asked. "What's happening?"

Without his helmet, he wouldn't have heard the message that they'd been fired on. Wright switched to external comm and explained. He added, "I really wish you would wear your helmet."

Arthur only smiled.

The ship swerved heavily, forcing everyone over to the side. Only the magnetic hold of their boots on the deck kept them standing. Had it been an evasive maneuver or the effect of a second hit? Not knowing what was going on was frustrating.

The *Defiant* swerved again and a tingle passed through Wright the like of which he'd never felt before.

"What was that?" Taylan asked.

"No id—"

"Hull breach Deck Two," Colbourn announced.

That was the deck directly above.

Wright asked, "Do you want me to do anything, Brigadier?"

"Not yet. A breach repair team has been dispatched."

Shit.

He chose to not relay the news to his men and women. There was nothing they could do about it anyway, and he needed them to focus.

Things were going the way they had on the shuttle. That had been breached before the tail section had been sliced off.

The atmosphere readings on his HUD altered. The breach had to be a big one. Unless it had…

He looked up and around.

A klaxon screamed out.

There it is!

A crack had appeared on the bulkhead. Microseconds later it had run to the overhead.

"Ma'am, the breach has spread to Deck One."

"We're on it, Wright. Another team is on its way. Maintain your position."

The same tingle he'd felt a moment ago coursed through his body again. Another hit. The aliens were not playing with them this time. They were set on destroying the ship.

"Hull breach Deck Four."

The passenger cabins were on Deck Three. Too late, Wright realized there was now no access to it with Two breached.

He glanced over his shoulder. Taylan was standing with the rear guard, her body armor and rifle identical to everyone else's yet to him she was unmistakable.

He couldn't see her face through her darkened visor but he felt her gaze meet his. "If you want to—"

"I know," she choked. "I'm talking to them now."

The crack in the hull was widening. Decompression started up. Arthur raised his hand as if feeling for wind direction. He seemed to struggle to breathe. The *Defiant* would auto-repair but not fast enough, and there was no sign of the team Colbourn had promised.

"Arthur, put on your helmet!"

The king steadfastly shook his head. "Is this it, TJ?"

The tingle hit Wright's body for a third time. "I think it might be."

Arthur appeared confused. "I did not think it would end like this. I should have died thousands of years ago. I do not mourn my ending. But it is wrong of Merlin to kill all of you as well."

The fissure in the bulkhead had spread. Wright could have pushed fingers into it. On the outer hull it was probably already centimeters wide. A breach team wouldn't arrive now. The section would have sealed. He ordered everyone to retreat to the farthest ends of the passageway and hold onto anything they could find. They were done for, but dying from asphyxiation was preferable to being pulled through a narrow gap.

Wright found Taylan. They stood with the Marines, pressed against the sealed doors, hand in hand.

A dropped weapon lazily rose to midair before being drawn to the breach.

The *Defiant* had lost gravity.

She was breaking up.

Arthur had not moved.

His legs outspread, he lifted Excalibur in one hand, his beard and mane of silver hair whipped by the gale of escaping gases. He grimaced and his chest heaved as he struggled to breathe.

Then he spoke, and Wright only just made out his words in the thinning air.

"Merlin, my old friend! Do not wreak your vengeance on my countrymen. They have done no wrong, only sought to protect their lands and loved ones, as you helped me to do long ago. If someone must die, let it be me. Allow the others to go free."

His plea drew no reaction. The tear in the hull continued to widen, the depressurization rush nearly pulling Arthur off his feet.

"Merlin!" the king screamed. "You saw something in me once, something you thought worth preserving for thousands of years. All my life we were friends and companions. If that meant anything to you, if *I* meant anything to you, I beg you, do not do this. Let my people live!"

With a resounding *crack*! the breach tore open. A jumble of bodies hurtled toward it, Wright's among them. Taylan's hand was ripped from his grasp. He'd lost her.

His visor smashed into someone's helmet and fractured. His suit alarm went off. A sharp hiss signaled escaping internal atmosphere.

Where was Taylan?

He was whirling, propelled into the void. He saw body armor, a rifle, a glimpse of Arthur, blackness, stars.

He was fading.

Where was Taylan?

Ah, he could see her now.

She was walking toward him wearing an ivory gown that swept the floor. It was like the dress Guinevere's ghost had worn on the *Dauntless*. She was holding a bouquet of wild daffodils and she had flowers in her hair. Kayla walked behind her, holding her train, and people sat in rows on each side, watching as she passed.

She smiled at him.

His vision blurred.

She was gone.

34

The first sensation to hit Taylan was weight. One moment she was spinning into the vacuum, forever torn from her kids and Wright, and the next she was inexplicably weighed down. Another heavy weight rested in her hand.

She blinked. Her view was narrow and oblong, as if she were looking through a slit. She could see colorful shapes against a green background. She tilted her head back. Above, the sky was blue and puffs of white cloud rode the air currents.

She could smell grass and something else, something earthy and sweaty.

A jangling sound came from one side. When she turned her head toward it, the shapes and greenness were replaced by...

She squinted.

Was that a *horse*?

She must be unconscious. She must have hit her head while being sucked through the hull breach. Or maybe this was some kind of dream as she was dying, her oxygen-deprived brain conjuring images from her past. She waited. Would she wake up or would the dream fade to blackness?

She wished she'd been able to see Patrin and Kayla one more time.

The dream continued.

In the absence of anything else to do, she decided she would go with it. She brought her free hand up to her face to find out what was blocking her vision. Her fingers met metal and, more than that, they felt as though they were covered in metal too. She opened and closed a fist experimentally. A soft clinking sound reached her ears, as if pieces of metal were rubbing together.

What was she holding in her other hand?

She angled the slit in front of her eyes downward and lifted her encumbered arm. She was so surprised at what she saw that her hand opened reflexively and she dropped the sword. The soft thud as it hit the ground told her she was standing on turf.

Everything began to add up: horse, sword, metal glove, green field, the feeling of being weighed down.

Leaving the sword where it was, she gingerly touched the covering on her face again and pushed it up. Her visor opened, and finally she could see.

Holy fuck.

This wasn't confusion after a head trauma and she wasn't dying. This was a hallucinogenic nightmare. Someone had slipped her some bad shit.

A green field ran from her feet to hills on the horizon, dotted with pavilions and tents in many colors. She stood among a group of knights in full armor. The ones who had also figured out how to open their visors looked as shocked and confused as she imagined she did. The horse she'd seen was one of several standing to her right, shifting from hoof to hoof. The jangling she'd heard had been the bells on their bridles.

Her pulse thumping in her ears, she tried to make sense of what she could see. She scanned the surroundings and realized they looked familiar. She was back on the alien planet. The topography was the same only it had been transformed to a scene from...

Where was Arthur?

Even more importantly, where were Patrin and Kayla, and where was Wright?

A knight fumbling with his visor caught her attention. Even clad in mail, he looked familiar. After picking up her sword, she stepped over to him and lifted the metal covering from his face.

"Taylan?!" Wright's expression of utter shock and surprise was almost comical as he took in the scene. Then he grabbed her into a rib-cracking hug. Finally, he said, "What the hell's going on?"

"Your guess is as good as mine. I'm just glad we aren't dead, or don't seem to be. I'm going to see if I can find the kids."

"I'll help you."

They were not too hard to spot in the end. A hulking knight in armor stood next to a maiden in a simple gown, her hair under a wimple. Taylan had never been so relieved to see her children, except possibly that time when she found them in the outback.

"Mam?" Kayla asked, peering at her. "Is that you?"

"Of course it is," Patrin answered. "Can't you tell?"

"I've never seen her dressed as a Knight of the Round Table before," Kayla retorted. "Is that what's going on? Have we gone back to Earth and Arthur's time?"

Patrin rolled his eyes. "How could that be true? We've been traveling through space for months."

"Well, if you're so clever, how do you explain this?" Kayla spread her arms wide.

"Where Merlin and Morgan are concerned anything's possible," said Taylan. "But I recognize this place. Don't you?"

"Yes, I do!" Patrin replied, his eyes widening.

"We're back where we were before," said Wright. "The

aliens must have decided not to kill us just yet. This is some sick fantasy they've put us in. They want to play with us a bit. Taylan, I need to find Colbourn and Yorkson and speak to the Marines to put their minds at ease."

"Good luck with that. I'll try to find Arthur and talk with the others."

Once she looked for him, the king was easy to spot. He'd taken off his helmet and his hair and beard cascaded over his armor. He was walking away from her. Telling Patrin and Kayla not to move a muscle, she ran after him.

When she caught up to him, however, he didn't stop.

"Arthur, wait a minute." She touched his arm.

He brushed her off like a fly.

"Arthur!"

He seemed transfixed by something.

Following his line of sight, she saw a horse—a monster of a horse. At its shoulder, the bay stallion stood not much shorter than Arthur's height. The animal wore mail and the Pendragon arms on its flanks and breast collar.

The king reached it and gently ran his hand over its cheek and jaw. The horse bowed its head, Arthur breathed into its nostrils, and its hoof gently scraped the ground. Reaching up, he held each side of its lowered head and pressed his forehead into the animal's blaze.

He turned to look at Taylan, his eyes wet. "He is my destrier. I know he isn't real, but..." He rested his head on the horse's once more and patted its neck.

"Arthur, how nice of you to visit."

Merlin had appeared out of nowhere.

Taylan took a step back.

Merlin continued, "I thought you might like to see another old friend of yours."

Arthur straightened up, taking hold of his horse's reins.

Tiny silver bells on the bridle jingled. "Thank you for bringing him to me, and for not killing my friends."

"Your thanks may be premature," Merlin replied, a twinkle in his eye. "As you can see, they all remain a long way from home and safety."

"Merlin," Taylan said, taking a step forward, "this game of yours has gone on long enough. Let us go home. Leave us alone. We aren't toys for you to play with. What you and your species does is disgusting."

"Ah yes, Lancelot's descendant. And I believe another generation in your family is here too."

Taylan felt the color drain from her face. He knew about Patrin and Kayla. But of course he did. He could probably see the connections running from her to her children like bees saw ultraviolet. She was blind in comparison.

The alien snickered. "What possible reason could I and my fellow players have for allowing you to leave and giving up our game?"

"So you can do what's decent and right."

"These are human concepts—interesting, but without value among my kind."

Taylan bit her lip. There had to be something that would appeal to him, something he would agree to in order to let them go free. "You could have killed us all a short while ago but you didn't. Whatever it was that changed your minds then, the same reasoning applies now. Let us go."

Please don't kill my children.

"I'm afraid you're wrong," Merlin replied. "That reasoning is why you're here. If we wished, we could return all of you to your little, backward planet in your equivalent of an instant. We will not be doing that. You dared to invade our system, to try to look into the eyes of your gods. For that, you all deserve to die. Arthur appealed to my sense of comradeship with him and I decided to grant a stay of execution, that's all. Perhaps there is still some entertainment to be had from you. The expressions on your faces when you found yourselves thrust back several thousand years has already fulfilled that criterion somewhat."

Taylan stared at him. How cruel and depraved could his species be? Arguments whirled around her mind but she couldn't hit on anything that might sway him. There was no point in asking for mercy, no point in telling him of Seren's pregnancy or her own children's youth. There was also nothing she could offer on Earth's behalf in exchange for their lives. Humans *had* nothing to offer this highly advanced life form, except, as Merlin put it, 'entertainment'.

Maybe that was it. "You've brought us here to fight for our lives, haven't you? That's what all this is about." She lifted the sword in her hand and indicated the field of knights and chargers.

"Well spotted," the alien replied sarcastically.

"I'm guessing our opponents will appear in a minute, phantasms of the kind Morgan made of my children, or maybe like the copies of you and her that attacked the *Dauntless*—for fun."

"Something like that." The corner of his lip lifted.

"We won't do it."

"Won't do what?"

"We'll refuse to fight."

"Taylan," Arthur demurred.

"Be quiet," she told him. To Merlin she said, "What's the point in fighting if we're going to die anyway? We might as well give up now. Literally fall on the swords you've so handily supplied. It'll make a bit of a mess of your nice field, but that's your problem. I'm sure you'll find a way to deal with it."

"Nonsense," said Merlin. "Humans would never give up so easily. That's what makes you so engaging."

"I'm telling you," she said, "if you want a fight worth watching you need to give us something worth fighting for."

The alien raised a finger to his lip. "Go on. I'm intrigued."

This was it. This was what floated their boats. They loved humanity's fierce grip on life. That was why they incited conflict. They got their kicks watching people fight it out. Maybe their long lives or even immortality had made them jaded, and seeing humans cling to life with every ounce of their being made *them* feel alive.

"We will fight if, when we win, you let us go and vow to never interfere in human affairs again."

"*When* you win?" Merlin asked. "Don't you mean if?"

"No, when," said Wright, who had suddenly arrived at Taylan's side. "We'll win if you give us a fair fight. Those are your rules, aren't they? You make things roughly equal. When you attacked the *Dauntless* your ship was a near-copy and you used pulse rifles against us. On Earth you made the two main pieces on each side of the game, Arthur and Kala Orr, impervious to harm."

"That is the essence of it." Merlin's eyes narrowed. "How astute. Perhaps you are a whole step above other primates after all."

"Give us an even chance of winning," Wright pressed, "and the rewards Taylan asked for, and we'll do it. Is that right, Taylan?"

"That's right. Those are our conditions."

35

───────

"No one gave you permission to negotiate with these lunatics," Yorkson seethed. "Just who do you think you are?"

The aliens had dressed him in some kind of merchant's or court administrator's costume, probably after correctly concluding he was too old to fight. He looked ridiculous. His floppy hat had fallen over one eye and his face was red with anger. The admiral was clearly out of his depth, and it showed.

"I think Taylan's got us the only break we're going to get," said Wright. "The aliens have no regard for human life. We're toys to them. If they get bored they'll break us and go on their way."

"If they have so little regard for human life," Yorkson countered, "what makes you so sure they'll hold to their word? We could fight their stupid battle and they could still kill us all anyway."

"We can't be sure," Taylan agreed, "but we're dead whatever we do. They nearly killed us on the *Defiant*. It was only Arthur pleading for our lives that's given us a stay of execution. For all Merlin's cold-heartedness, he seems to feel just a tiny bit of affection for our king and fond memories of their time together. Look around you. He's recreated Arthur's time in perfect detail. If there's the smallest chance we can exploit his feelings of friendship and nostalgia, we should take it."

Colbourn seemed undecided on the question. The aliens had made her a knight, and she studied her gauntlets thoughtfully, opening and closing her hands.

Almost everyone was a knight. All the Marines, the brothers from West BI, Abacha, Captain Ford, and Kevin all wore mail and carried swords. Only a few of the mission members were not knights, and aside from Yorkson they were all women. Iolani, Kekoa, and Seren wore long gowns and wimples like Kayla's. The engineer, Krol, a friend of Wright's from the *Resolute*, was also in a dress, and she looked furious about it.

Taylan didn't know what had happened to Kala Orr and Perran. They seemed to have disappeared.

"Admiral," Colbourn said, "unfortunate at it may be, I don't believe we have any choice about it. For better or worse, Ellis has agreed terms with the aliens on our behalf, even though she lacked the authority." She gave Taylan a withering glance. "We can't back out now, especially as we don't have any better ideas."

"But a full-on battle in the ancient style?" Yorkson asked, his pitch high. "With swords, and horses, and—"

"This isn't really how it would have been," Taylan interrupted. "There would have been unarmored infantry too, recruited from the local peasants, and archers."

"Well, thank you for the history lesson," Yorkson said icily. "That's a *great* help. My point is, we have no idea what we're doing. My men and women are not knights, they are Royal Marines." He whipped off his hat and used to to mop his sweaty brow. He continued in a calmer tone. "I have no idea how to command them. I'm not familiar with the battle tactics of the olden times. How should the troops be positioned? How should they move over the course of the battle? I simply don't know."

Taylan didn't answer. The admiral's worries were valid and she didn't know how to help him. She'd never studied the battles of ancient times in any detail either. She'd always been more interested in one-on-one combat and the stories of the famous knights.

"As I understand it," said Wright, "it's kind of like a game of chess. You have the king, who the other side tries to capture and kill, knights on horseback, who have more maneuverability than most of the rest of the pieces, foot sold—"

Taylan grabbed his arm. "Yes, it *is* like chess. It's also like xiangqi."

She left to find Abacha.

THE KNIGHTS ON THE ALIENS' side seemed just about identical to the Alliance's. Their faces were invisible behind their visors but the number of them was the same. They had the same amount of horses too. They'd appeared suddenly and silently on the open field beyond the tents.

"How much longer do we have?" Abacha asked, looking nervously at the enemy.

"I don't know," said Taylan. "Knowing Merlin, he won't give us much notice."

Abacha returned his attention to the patch of dirt at his feet, where he'd been scratching maneuvers. "It's fairly simple anyway. Simpler than xiangqi as we only have three types of pieces: the general, soldiers, and horses. No cannon, advisors, or elephants."

"Elephants!" exclaimed Yorkson. "No, thank the stars."

"I suggest our right flank moves first, advancing the horses. How many riders do we have?"

"I'm not sure," Taylan replied. Several Marines had taken charge of horses. She hoped there were enough of them.

Abacha said, "The enemy is likely to mirror our advance. What we do next depends on what they do with their general, if he enters the fight or if he hangs back."

"Their general?" Yorkson asked.

"Their king. Knowing Arthur, our king will fight."

"I wouldn't like to try to stop him," Taylan commented.

Arthur had already been up on his destrier practicing swings with Excalibur.

"So he'll be in the thick of it," said Abacha. "Will the enemy try to cut a line straight through to him or will they go for easier targets first? Namely, us."

A painful silence fell. The bizarre situation was most likely everyone's last taste of life. Taylan pushed the thought away. She could accept her own death but not the deaths of the people she loved. "If their king hangs back, we should try a pincer movement, sending our fastest and best fighters around each side to attack him while the rest of our troops keep theirs too busy to notice."

Abacha smiled. "You did learn something from our xiangqi games after all."

"*Will* any of you be able to kill him?" asked Yorkson. "Wasn't there some talk of Arthur being indestructible? If their king is a mirror image he'll have the same protection."

"I don't think Arthur is indestructible anymore," Wright replied. "He took a hit at Mars Station. First time I've known it. Merlin may have removed his protection. On the other hand, he didn't have Excalibur with him, so I'm not sure."

Taylan said, "Excalibur was only ever meant to prevent him from dying from a wound. The invulnerability to pulse fire was a new thing." She sighed. "We just don't know. We'll have to hope we can kill their king."

"And that Merlin doesn't pull a fast one at the last minute," said Wright. "We can't trust him to play fair."

"You're right," said Iolani, who had just joined them. She peered at Abacha's scratchings in the dirt. "Is this the battle plan?"

"Just some ideas," Abacha replied.

"Can *you* give us any insights into what we might expect?" Taylan asked.

Iolani shrugged. "I would love to. That's why I came over. But, thinking about it, this seems to be more of a military exercise than anything. I do agree with Wright, though. You shouldn't expect the aliens to play by the rules they agreed. That would be expecting them to behave like humans—humans with a modicum of integrity. They aren't human, and they've already shown they see us as little more than animals. You could do everything right, win the battle, and kill or capture their king, and the aliens might still go back on everything you've agreed."

Taylan said, "That's a chance we'll have to take."

36

Wright looked up into the blue sky and then out over the green fields to the surrounding hills. The aliens had created a reasonable facsimile of Earth. Or were they only projecting the scenery into his mind? It was impossible to tell.

Even though it wasn't Earth, it was a good place to die. Better than suffocating to death in an EVA suit in the freezing, lifeless vacuum of space.

Merlin's knights began to advance. They walked like automata, their armor glinting in the sunlight.

Yorkson would soon give the signal to go out to meet them, but Taylan was still arguing with Patrin, trying to get him to dismount his horse and not participate in the battle. He'd taken a position at Arthur's side among the small contingent of mounted knights.

Taylan's anxious, loud tones floated across the field on the wind. There was no way she would get Patrin to agree and her son was too big and strong to be physically forced. Everyone seemed to know it but her as they all ignored the argument.

The men from West BI stood a little down the line to

Wright's left. Captain Ford was farther on, near the end. The other Australian, Kevin, stood with him. Abacha would remain at Yorkson's side to help direct the battle—unless they decided to implement Taylan's suggestion, in which case he would join the fastest runners.

Wright could not imagine running in this armor. Maybe he would manage a fast jog.

A piercing whistle shrilled through the air.

It was time.

He began to walk toward the enemy, his feet falling heavy on the soft ground. The line advanced with him. Taylan raced behind the walking knights until she reached his side. Her face was wet and her eyes teary. She joined him, and her jaw set grimly before she lowered her visor.

Muttered curses leaked from within her helmet, then she said, louder, "He wouldn't listen! He's a kid. Just a kid. He thinks he's in a fairy tale."

"You tried," he replied. "What he does is up to him. Where's Kayla?"

"With the women. They found a tent full of bandages, splints, and stretchers, and they got the message they're supposed to tend the wounded. The real medics have joined them. Patrin should have stayed with his sister. I need him to protect her."

"I'm not sure that'll help if things go against us."

"Shut up," said Taylan. "Just shut up." Then, barely audibly, "I hate it when you make sense."

He cast a glance down the line. Despite the danger and the hopeless situation and the sheer lunacy of it all, his heart filled with awe and admiration. The mounted knights on their mail-coated horses, coats of arms in bright colors adorning their flanks, looked magnificent. A battle standard had been found, and Arthur's dragon floated high and proud. On each side of the mounts, knights in gleaming armor walked steady and unflinching toward their fate.

In modern warfare, humans killed at a distance. Pulse rifles, mortars, heavy guns, rockets, laser fire, drone attacks, missiles, bombs—these all killed, but the deaths and injuries were not personal. Rarely did the occasion arise when you had to stick a knife in someone, to feel it go in and see the effect of what you were doing on the victim's face. Killing like that took guts. His own experiences of death close-up had scarred him. Arthur's knights had been brave men to go willingly into battle.

The distance between the two sides was closing uncomfortably fast.

"Keep your shield up and stay close to me," Taylan said, tension edging her voice.

"Don't worry, I'm not stupid."

Apart from Arthur, she was the best sword-fighter they had.

The tramp of metal-shod feet was loud, laced with the thuds of horses' hooves. The noise re-doubled as the enemy drew nearer.

Would they be as easy to kill as ordinary men? More importantly, would they stay dead or dissolve into smoke as the Merlins and Morgans on the *Dauntless* had, rejuvenating and returning for another go? If that happened, his side was screwed. There was no fire-extinguishing system here.

A shout rang out. The mounted knights kicked their steeds to a trot, and the small group broke from the line. The trot quickly became a canter, and then a gallop. The battle standard streamed out.

The enemy's cavalry charged out to meet Arthur and his men, leaving their foot soldiers behind. The mounted knights barreled into them with a great clash of arms. The two sides began to hack at each other, their horses rearing and neighing, bringing down their iron shoes on the necks of their foes.

"Here we go," said Taylan.

The walking knights began to run. A roar ran down the line. Wright found himself roaring too, as he and Taylan lifted their swords and rushed into battle.

Coming up against the knight opposite him was like hitting a brick wall. He struggled against the thing's shield, trying to get a hit in with his sword.

An agony of confusion followed.

Armored bodies were everywhere, pushing, shoving, clashing. Swords cut through the air, but there was no space to slice or thrust. His helmet took a blow, making his ears ring. There were shouts, yells, screams. He couldn't make out what was being said. He tried to find Taylan, but the narrow view through his visor showed only a wave-tossed sea of mail, shields, and helmets. Something thrust into his side, sending pain shooting through his ribs. Another blow clanged against his helmet, setting his ears ringing louder and pain exploding in his head. He swung about and blindly attacked. He was quickly growing tired, weakening with the effort of moving in armor, holding up his shield, and lifting the heavy sword. Ages seemed to pass, though it was probably only minutes.

Just as he felt he couldn't take any more, suddenly, somehow, he broke free from the throng, amazed to discover empty air surrounding him. He staggered backward, panting, and lifted his visor. Many knights were already down, lying still or groaning, their blood oozing into the grass. Medics were loading one man onto a stretcher, while Iolani was bravely staying put in the midst of the battle as she tried to staunch another man's wounds. But there were so many wounded. Too many for the helpers to attend.

Colbourn was hurt.

Her helmet had come off and her cropped white hair was stained red. As he darted toward her, a knight ran at him, sword aloft. Wright swept his blade into the thing's visor, delivering a deep dent. It cried out and fell face downward.

A riderless horse galloped across his path, and then Wright was on his way again. The clang and clatter of metal on metal, the yells of the fighters, and the cries of the wounded were so loud it was hard to think.

He reached the brigadier and sank to his knees. Her skin was chalky white and her eyes closed. Was she already dead? Was that why no one was helping her? If only he could see her status on a HUD.

Her eyes fluttered open, and then snapped wide as she gawped at something over his shoulder.

He ducked.

A blade cut through the place his head had been. He dropped to the side, rolled onto his back, and thrust his sword upward. He'd had no time to aim, but by chance the tip found the gap below his attacker's helmet and passed straight through it, sinking deep into its head. The sickening feeling of blade piercing flesh came through to Wright's hand. He jerked the sword free and blood gushed out as the knight toppled onto him. It was only a creation of the aliens, yet he felt its death.

Heaving off the heavy, lifeless body took all his strength as he bore the weight of its armor as well as his own.

"Get back to the fight," Colbourn groaned. "I've had it."

"No, I'll get you help." He scanned the battlefield. There was Kekoa, running to Iolani, her arms full of bandages.

He shouted her name, got her attention, and then pointed at Colbourn. When he'd seen her nod of acknowledgment, he said to the brigadier, "Someone's on their way. Hold on."

He climbed to his feet. It was time to return to the melee.

But who should he fight?

In the tussle of armored bodies, it was hard to tell who was friend and who was foe.

A shriek went up, so intense and full of pain for a second everything seemed to pause, then the fighting resumed.

The cry had come from the wife of one of the men from

West BI. She knelt in the field over a body, her pregnant belly filling out her gown. The cacophony of the battle drowned out her continuing cries of grief and agony. Her mouth screamed in silence while she rocked forward and backward, tearing at her clothes and hair.

Time seemed to slow and the noise of the battle receded.

Beyond the knights who fought on foot, the mounted knights continued to hack at and harry each other. Blood ran down their horses' legs and spattered to the ground, now churned mud. Arthur sat tall in the middle, Excalibur flashing.

Wright stood mesmerized by the sight, so strange on this alien planet.

"There you are." Taylan's helmet and shield were covered in dents and scratches, but she appeared uninjured. "Come on, we're going for their king. He's over there."

She pointed at a lone figure on horseback, slowly leaving the scene of battle.

Then she noticed the pregnant woman weeping over her husband's corpse.

She froze.

"*Marc.*"

Wright touched her shoulder. "I'm sorry. I know he was your friend."

Something between a gasp and sob escaped from Taylan, then she said in a strangled tone, "We have to get their king."

But as she spoke, Arthur broke from the chaos of his fight. Excalibur was in one of his hands and in his other he carried the pole from which his battle standard flew. His horse cantered to an open patch of grass, he lifted the standard high, and then he dashed it to the ground.

"What's that about?" asked Wright.

"I think Arthur just surrendered."

37

─────────

When the clash of armor and blades had ended, the only sounds were of wounded knights moaning in agony and the wails of the grieving widow. Taylan pulled off her helmet, and suddenly the sounds became louder as the cool air hit her wet skin. Along with the post-battle noise came the scent of blood and death.

She was tired, body, heart, and soul. Tired of years of fighting the EAC, the long search for her children, and the endless conflict with the aliens.

Poor Marc.

Poor Seren.

She wiped her blade on the grass and returned it to its scabbard.

At least Wright seemed okay. Now the battle was over he'd also removed his helmet and returned his attention to Colbourn, who'd taken a hit. He was kneeling by the brigadier's side.

Taylan scanned the field. There was Patrin. He seemed unhurt. He and Arthur were riding toward the tents. And there was Kayla, the hem of her skirt bloody.

Taylan winced. The days of her daughter's childhood were over.

Wright stood up and said, "She wants to talk to you."

"Colbourn wants to talk to *me*? Why?" What could the woman who had hated her existence have to say to her?

"Please," Wright said, "just listen."

She crouched down near the brigadier's head. She looked like shit. Between the smears of drying blood, her skin was alabaster. Her lips moved but Taylan couldn't make out any words. She leaned closer, putting her ear to Colbourn's mouth.

"Might have been wrong about you…" she whispered. "Saw your potential…Thought it was wasted…Wright's a good man… Look after him."

When the brigadier said nothing else, Taylan turned to peer at her. Colbourn's gaze was fixed and still.

She stood up.

Wright was looking down at the fallen officer. From the look on his face, she didn't need to tell him anything.

"I'm sorry."

He nodded, his lips pressed into a line. He cleared his throat and squinted at the horizon. "What now?"

"Now we find out what the fuck's going on."

Arthur and Patrin had dismounted and were slowly walking their horses off the field. Taylan jogged with Wright to meet them.

"Patrin, are you all right?"

"I'm okay, Mam. Just a few bruises."

"What's happening, Arthur?" she asked. "Why did you give up?"

The king regarded her wearily. His surcoat was bloody and slashed, and his horse seemed to struggle to put one hoof in front of the other. "The battle was lost, Taylan. I put a stop to the bloodshed."

"But…" She was about to say, *We're going to die anyway* but the words wouldn't leave her lips, not while her son was right in front of her.

"He's right," Patrin said. "It's easier to see what's going on when you're on horseback. Our side was losing by a long way."

"But if we'd killed their king," she said, "it wouldn't have mattered."

Arthur replied, "You could not have killed their king."

"Why not? We could have tried." The hopelessness of their situation hit her and she protested in anguish, "You should have let us try!"

"Mam," Patrin said angrily, "you don't know who it was."

"Taylan Ellis," said a smooth voice behind her.

Merlin wore armor and a surcoat like Arthur's, except his was not cut or besmirched. He was without his horse, but she immediately recognized him as the mounted figure who had been walking away from the fighting.

"Thank you for the idea of getting you to fight for your freedom," he said. "It certainly added frisson to your struggle. I hope you don't mind me taking part in the battle personally, to experience your striving for life at close quarters. Shame it didn't work out for you."

"You have to let us try again," said Wright. "That wasn't fair. If the king on your side was indestructible, you didn't play according to your own rules."

"How do you know Arthur isn't indestructible too?" Merlin asked.

"Because he was hurt by pulse fire on Mars Station."

"But I could have returned his invulnerability to him. How do you know I didn't?"

Merlin's face was a picture of sardonic amusement. He was enjoying himself, playing with them. They would never know whether Arthur could have been killed in the battle unless one of them tried to do it, and of course no one would.

"This isn't it!" Taylan exclaimed. "It isn't over yet. There has to be more. Another chance. Give us another chance!"

Merlin's eyes drank in her desperation thirstily.

"My friend," Arthur's tone was soft and pleading "there has to be another way."

"There is."

Morgan had finally appeared. Walking from one of the tents, she wore the same long, dark gown she'd worn on Earth. Kala and Perran Orr followed in her wake.

"Why let everything end now when we're having so much fun?" she asked.

"I see you've brought your brood with you," Merlin said. "How predictable."

"Why shouldn't I keep my little ones close? Taylan Ellis understands a mother's love. Don't you, dear?"

Taylan shuddered.

Kala Orr was looking supremely pissed off, no doubt recalling her horrific torture at Morgan's hands, but she had the good sense to keep her mouth shut. Of all the humans, she and her son were most likely to survive in the current circumstances.

"That's why you want to prolong this game," said Merlin to Morgan, his lip curling. "You've grown sentimentally attached to your half-breed descendants. Revolting. It should be against the rules to breed with the pieces."

"You should try it some time," said Morgan archly. "It might loosen you up a bit."

"I would never—"

"I agree it's too soon for the fun to be over," she interrupted. "I know what you should do next. A joust. You against Arthur."

Her fellow alien opened his mouth to speak but then shut it again, his expression pensive. He was considering the idea.

"I am willing to do it," said Arthur. "It's an excellent suggestion. But if I defeat you, you must allow us to depart."

"And leave Earth alone for eternity," Taylan added.

"And you have to keep your word," said Wright. "No tricks or last-minute changes of gameplay."

Ignoring the humans' words, Merlin said to Morgan, "You understand me too well."

A look passed between them that nauseated Taylan, and she pulled a face at Wright. Despite the dire situation, he smiled.

"Think of it," said Morgan. "It will be like old times. Knight against knight, each pitting the best of their skills against the other. Only this time it'll be you in the saddle, something you couldn't do before. You against Arthur, King of the Britons."

Merlin looked the king up and down. He surveyed the blood-stained field, where wounded knights continued to receive treatment while others lay still, beyond help. He turned back to face Morgan. "Agreed."

Taylan slumped with relief. They would not die just yet.

"I will ready myself," said Arthur. Pulling his horse's bridle, he walked away.

Neither Merlin nor Morgan had stated a time for the joust to begin. There was nothing Taylan could do to help Arthur prepare. She knew little about horses, let alone jousting, so she asked Patrin to go with her and Wright to find Kayla. If Arthur failed, at least her family would be together at the end.

"All right," Patrin agreed. "Give me a minute." He tied his horse's reins to a tent post.

"Was it bad in the battle?" she asked as they walked.

Patrin shrugged. "I did okay. I fought like you taught me, and I had no trouble with my horse after Arthur's lessons."

Though his tone was light, he had the look of someone who had seen too much, the same look as Wright often wore.

A visceral hatred of the aliens who had brought so much pain and untimely death to humans gripped her. She promised herself that if Arthur lost, she would inflict all the damage she could on Merlin and Morgan before they took her out.

"*No,*" Wright murmured.

He'd halted next to a body. The man had been around Wright's age, maybe a tad younger. His sightless eyes stared skyward.

"It's Ford," Wright explained dully, "from the *Resolute.*"

Taylan recalled the cheeky Australian who had teased Kevin in the gym. Though it seemed impossible, her heart sank further. Where was Kevin? Had he survived?

"Mam!" Kayla barreled into her and enveloped her in a tight hug. "I thought you might be dead!"

"I'm fine," she said, returning her daughter's embrace. "Are you okay?"

"It's been horrible, horrible." Kayla's face was tear-streaked and her hands soiled with dirt and blood.

"It should be over soon," Taylan said. "Arthur and Merlin are going to joust. Then we can go home."

Wright gave her a questioning look but said nothing.

What did he want her to tell her daughter? That if Arthur lost they were all going to die?

38

———————

Taylan's friend, Kevin, was alive. That was something Wright was thankful for. The Australian had received a cut to his neck that looked bad, but the medic said it wasn't near major blood vessels and he should survive.

How long Kevin and everyone else had to live was another question. Everything hung on Merlin and Arthur's joust, and even if Arthur won, there was no guarantee the aliens would uphold their end of the bargain. They were entirely at their mercy, but it was the best that could be done.

Merlin lifted an arm and drew his hand along the horizontal plane. As if springing from his fingertips, a jousting list appeared, roughly 150 meters long. A wooden barrier hung with brightly decorated cloths separated the two sides, lances protruding from barrels at each end. The rectangular section was enclosed by rope barriers.

The battle survivors began to gather.

Arthur walked to his horse, heavy-footed and shoulders down, his helmet under his arm. His once-lustrous silver hair hung in rat tails, brown with blood, and the lines of old age cut deep in his face.

"Can he do it?" Wright asked Taylan.

She didn't answer.

Merlin's gait was sprightly as he strode to his steed and grabbed the reins before climbing easily into the saddle. He kicked the horse sharply. It whinnied and reared, and bright red drops ran from the spots where Merlin's spurs had pierced it. Another kick and the horse trotted through an opening to the list.

Arthur's horse seemed to sink lower when he mounted it, clearly weary from the battle and its master's weight. He slipped his helmet over his head, leaned forward and whispered into the animal's ear, lovingly stroking its neck. Horse and rider walked slowly to the opposite end of the wooden barrier from Merlin.

He's too old. Too tired.

Wright took Taylan's hand and they stepped up to the ropes. Morgan, Kala Orr, and her son stood at the opposite side of the list at the center. Small noises from the audience faded until the only sound was the wind in the grass.

Arthur had reached the end of the barrier. He lowered his visor, grasped a lance, and lifted it out of the barrel, balancing the end under his arm. With his other arm, he shifted his shield in front of his body. His horse moved restlessly under him.

At the other end of the barrier, Merlin did the same.

The two riders waited for the signal.

What was it to be?

Morgan reached into her sleeve and drew out a handkerchief. Her gaze moving from rider to rider, she lifted it high. Seconds passed. In the audience, all movement ceased.

Morgan released the handkerchief.

As it fluttered downward on the breeze, both horses were already thundering down the list. The knights' lances bounced and swayed but kept mainly true, aimed at the approaching rider.

"Come on, Arthur," Taylan muttered. "You can do it."

Shouts of encouragement came from the onlookers "*Arthur, Arthur, Arthur!*" until the chant match the beat of the horses' hooves, their great strides carrying their masters to their destiny.

Arthur leaned forward in his saddle, his shield high as he braced for the impact. His lance was straight as an arrow as he neared Merlin, the long years of practice evident in every part of his being.

But Merlin's positioning matched his in every detail. The alien did not need to train to perform this feat. Somehow, he'd stolen the skill and made it his own.

Taylan's grip on Wright's hand tightened. "*Come on!*"

The lances smashed into the shields.

Almost too fast to see, Arthur's lance burst apart, sending splinters flying. Merlin's held, hitting Arthur's shield square on. The force drove him from his saddle. He flew off his horse and landed in the dirt, his armor jangling.

The king seemed dazed. At first, he didn't move, only lay on his side.

Meanwhile, Merlin had circled his horse around and was walking it back to the spot where Arthur lay recovering from his unseating.

The king pulled himself to a sitting position and then to his feet.

"Is that it?" Wright asked. "Have we lost?"

"I'm not sure," Taylan replied. "I don't think so. Not yet."

But whatever happened, it wasn't looking good. Arthur was in bad shape.

Merlin pulled on his horse's reins, slowing it to a halt before dismounting.

"What's happening?" asked Wright.

"I think they're going to fight."

Merlin kicked the barrier, breaking the wood, until he could step through it.

Arthur drew Excalibur, crouched in a fighting position, his shield up, and waited.

Taylan said, "It looks like we're going to find out if Arthur's still invulnerable."

Wright had a feeling Merlin had withdrawn his protection. The alien was hard to read, but he seemed to be ambivalent about his attachment to the king. He was fond of him but only in the way an owner is fond of his pet, and even that feeling was fickle. And he also had a malevolent streak that meant he would relish putting Arthur down.

Merlin confidently strode the final few paces to his opponent. He circled Arthur, and the king turned in a smaller circle, following him.

Merlin lunged. Arthur parried, the clash of swords ringing out over the field. As Merlin's arm swept wide, Arthur moved in, bringing his blade down in an arc. But his opponent lifted his shield in time so Excalibur thunked into the solid wood. The king tried to wrench his sword free but it was stuck fast. Merlin dragged him forward and brought his own sword back, clapping the blade into Arthur's helmet.

The devastation of the blow was clear. Arthur fell to one side and onto his knees. Merlin tossed his shield away, wrenching Excalibur from Arthur's clasp. The king lifted his shield, but Merlin kicked it to one side and pinned the arm holding it under his boot. Arthur was defenseless.

"Stop!" Taylan cried out. "Mercy!"

Heedless of her plea, Merlin drove his blade into the king's armpit, where there was a gap in his armor. Arthur screamed. Merlin released his grip on his weapon and Arthur collapsed, half the sword sticking out of him.

The alien turned and lifted his fists in victory.

But there were no cheers, only a sullen, stunned silence.

Merlin had killed the King of the Britons, the Alliance's champion, and the savior of humankind.

Taylan's breathing was ragged. Wright could not believe it either.

It was finally all over.

Kala Orr stepped forward from Morgan's side, crossed the list, and walked through the gap in the barrier. When she reached Arthur, she pushed him with her foot.

He groaned. He was still alive, but not for much longer. No one could survive a wound like that.

Kala Orr pursed her lips and spat on the dying king.

She faced Merlin. "I and my son are only half human. We are of Morgan's blood. You can't treat us the same as these other wretches. We demand life."

"You *demand*?" Merlin asked softly.

"We...ask."

"But what will you do? Where will you go? The humans' ship is destroyed."

"We will remain here and live among you. We are your half-kin after all."

Perran raced across to the broken barrier. "*Mother...*"

"What?" She regarded him haughtily.

He was silent.

It was certainly a hard choice. Die now or remain trapped on a world populated by aliens and one lunatic parent.

"An interesting idea," said Merlin. "Morgan?"

His fellow alien shrugged disinterestedly. "If you like."

Her mother's love seemed to be rapidly evaporating. If Merlin agreed, Kala and Perran's lives would not be pleasant. A quick death would at least be painless.

"Very well," Merlin said. "You two may remain. For now."

Perran slumped to the ground, his head in his hands.

Kala turned triumphantly to Taylan. "You'll never kill me now, bitch."

But Taylan was beyond caring about the former Dwyr's petty vengeance. For the first time since Wright had known her, she looked utterly defeated. And he knew it was not because she faced her own death but because she'd brought her children to this place and so sealed their fate.

Merlin raised a hand. "As for the rest of you—"

"Wait!" a voice shouted.

Wright recognized it and scanned for the speaker. While Orr had been negotiating her survival, Patrin had gone under the rope barrier and grabbed the reins of Arthur's horse.

"Fight me."

"*You*?" Merlin took a second to realize who he was speaking to. "Ah yes, Lancelot's descendant. How touching you should come to Arthur's aid, but, as you can see, it's too late."

The king's chest was barely moving under his armor.

"Fight me," Patrin insisted, "you damned coward. You took on an old man. You stopped keeping Arthur young and vital years ago. He was no match for you and you knew it. Fight me. Or don't you dare?"

"Patrin!" Taylan yelled. "NO!"

"Let him have a go," Wright said. "What do we have to lose?"

"You want him to end up like that?" She jabbed a finger at Arthur as he lay dying.

Patrin had released the reins. He marched up to Merlin and slammed the hilt of his sword into his shield. "Fight me, dammit."

Taylan stepped toward the ropes. "Patrin…"

Wright reached out and grabbed her arm.

Her son screamed in Merlin's face, "Fight me, you c—!"

Taylan whirled around and slammed her fist into Wright's jaw. He dropped like a stone onto his butt, stars swimming in his vision. As he struggled to hold onto consciousness, he heard Merlin say, his tone full of menace, "*If* you insist."

WRIGHT RUBBED his jaw and blinked. He was seeing clearly again. Medics were removing Arthur on a stretcher and Patrin was walking the king's horse to the far end of the barrier. Merlin was also preparing to joust again.

Taylan looked down at him sorrowfully. "I'm sorry for hitting you, but Patrin's going to get himself killed." She held out her hand.

He took it and stood up. "I'm not sure what difference it makes now."

"Maybe none, but I can't bear to watch him die."

"It might not come to that."

"What do you mean? He doesn't stand a chance."

Wright hadn't meant that Patrin might win, rather that if he wasn't killed instantly he wouldn't be forced to linger. Merlin's patience had grown thin and he would put an end to all of them quickly once the fight was over.

"I don't know where he learned that word," Taylan muttered. "It wasn't from me."

He had more than a strong feeling it *was* from her.

She suddenly clasped his arm.

He flinched.

"Don't worry, I wasn't going to hit you again. I just thought of something. But... Damn!" She rose onto her tiptoes and peered at her son's end of the list. "It's too late to speak to Patrin."

"What?" Wright asked.

She bit her lip and said quietly, "It probably won't work, but it's worth a try."

Morgan had retrieved her handkerchief from the ground. She held it aloft again. Though it seemed impossible, the silence and stillness that instantly fell on the field was tenser than it had been before.

The cloth dropped from her fingertips, and the riders kicked their steeds into motion.

Taylan held out her hands in front of her and watched Merlin like a hawk.

Wright had no idea what she was doing but he hoped to hell it worked.

She spared one glance to the left, where Patrin raced down the list, his speed matching Merlin's, then she devoted all her focus to the alien.

His lance was up and steady, bouncing only slightly with the beat of his horse's gallop. His position was solid, his aim true. Unless Patrin was very lucky, the clash would go down as it had before, with him unseated. Then, would Patrin beat him in a sword fight? His chances were supposed to be even, but it was clear the alien had hedged everything in his own favor.

Merlin was only meters away, his mount's flanks flicking foam at every stride.

In the last seconds before lance met shield, Taylan smacked her cupped hands together, clapping loudly and yelling.

Patrin did not waver a millimeter, but Merlin's head turned toward the sound. His shield dropped a fraction and so did his lance. As its point hit Patrin's shield it glanced off it harmlessly, but Patrin's lance slipped into the gap above Merlin's.

It pierced the alien's throat.

Impaled on his attacker's weapon he was lifted from his horse, which galloped on without him. Perhaps in shock, Patrin didn't drop his lance at first but rode on several meters, Merlin dangling from it. Then he appeared to come to his senses. The weapon slipped from his grasp and the alien tumbled to the ground.

The audience stared in horror and amazement. Merlin appeared to still be alive. His hands clutched wildly at the implement in his throat and attempted to pull it out, though without success. The wooden spear was firmly embedded and protruding from the back of his neck. Merlin gagged and choked, his legs feebly twitching.

Morgan tittered.

Giving up his attempt to extract the lance, Merlin dissolved. His body and armor became fluid and oozed from around it, the colors and shapes mixing. Then the puddle slid to one side and quickly reformed to solidity. The alien stood up and shook himself like a wet dog.

While all this had been going on, Patrin trotted back on Arthur's horse. Peering down from his lofty height, he said, "Don't make me fight you. I won that fair and square."

"Hardly fair," Merlin said bitterly, his angry gaze turning to Taylan.

"I thought fairness and decency didn't matter to your species," she retorted. "Anyway, you did the same to me once. I thought I'd return the favor."

Morgan had walked out into the list once more. "*I* think it was all very amusing. A wonderful few moments' entertainment, don't you think?" She was addressing Merlin.

He scowled, but then he said grudgingly, "I suppose so."

"I have an idea. We could let them go and stop playing our game on Earth—if we receive something in return."

"No!" Taylan exclaimed. "We won. Patrin beat you."

"That is correct," Yorkson said. He'd run over to join in the discussion and was out of breath. "We won the wager. You have to fulfill your end of the bargain."

"We don't *have to* do anything at all," Morgan sneered. "I suggest you be quiet if you wish to live."

Yorkson's mouth snapped shut.

Merlin said, "The original agreement was about the battle. You lost. The rest was just for fun."

"We lost because you cheated," Wright said. "You powered up the opposition. We didn't stand a chance."

"Prove it," said Merlin.

"Stop bickering," Morgan complained. "It's very boring. I admit my estimation of your species has risen a little over the course of these events. Perhaps it would be better for us to leave you alone and allow you to develop unhindered by our games. In several hundred thousand of your years, humans may rise to a level worthy of our acquaintance. My proposition is this: two of you remain here so that we may study human thoughts and behavior in depth. The rest of you can go back."

"That's easy," Taylan said. "Kala and her son have already said they want to stay. And, to be honest, we'll be glad to be rid of them."

Perran interjected, "But I didn't—"

"Exactly," Kala said. "If the opportunity to return to Earth exists..."

"Be quiet," said Morgan. "You made your choice." Turning to Yorkson, she continued, "We need pure-bred humans. And I'm not asking you to decide which ones. I've already chosen. We'll take Arthur and the boy. They're clearly the best you have and we only want the best."

"*No*," Taylan breathed, turning pale. "Not my son. You're not taking my son."

"Good choices," Merlin commented. "I'm liking this idea more and more."

"There's no need for alarm," said Morgan. "It will only be for a little while."

"No," Taylan repeated firmly. "Not for all humanity. He won't stay here. I'm taking him home."

While the conversation had been going on, Patrin had dismounted and walked back. He'd been watching and listening silently. "Mam, I'll—"

"Marc!" a voice screamed.

The pregnant woman who had been grieving her husband's death in the battle raced across the field, to where a man was emerging from a tent.

It was him. The dead man had come back to life.

She raced into his arms and clung to him. Her cries of joy could be heard even at the distance.

"You could have them all back," Merlin said dismissively. "Arthur's already better. I'll bring the rest of them back to life in return for the boy."

"No!" Taylan's tone was desperate. She looked at Wright, her eyes pleading.

"How could you do this?!" screamed Perran, glaring at his mother. "You've ruined my life from the day I was born, and now I'll be stuck here with you forever."

"How dare you!" Kala retorted. "I've only ever tried to do my best for you, you ungrateful brat."

"Your best?" Perran lifted an arm and spun in a circle. "*This* is your best? We're in hell, and it's all your fault." He launched himself at Kala and fastened his hands around her neck.

Morgan and Merlin looked on, amused.

No one seemed particularly motivated to intervene, but then Meilyr strode over to the struggling pair and punched Perran's head. The force of his metal-clad knuckles knocked the boy out. As he sprawled unconscious on the grass Kala stepped carefully away from her son, rubbing her throat. She looked appealingly at the crowd, but attention had returned to the aliens and their demand.

"Mam," said Patrin, laying a gentle hand on Taylan's arm. "It's all right. I'll stay. I don't mind. I'm interested in this place, and they said it's only for a little while."

"You don't understand," she protested. "A short time to them is thousands of years to us. We'll never see each other again. It'll be like you died. You can't do this. I won't let you."

"Not at all," said Morgan. "We understand how fleeting your lives are, and I know all about maternal feelings. I would not do that to you, my dear."

Taylan looked daggers at her. "You don't know the first thing about being a mother, you evil witch. Stay out of my life."

Morgan's lip lifted in a sneer. "The boy, and you can all go home with a guarantee we won't bother humans again."

Patrin said, "It seems a small price to pay to get everyone who died brought back to life."

Taylan buried her head in Wright's chest as sobs wracked her. "I can't do it. Don't let them make me do it."

He held her close, not knowing what to say.

39

───────

Elek faced the crowd as it surged like a stormy sea. He raised his hands over his head, and quiet began to spread.

"Shhh!" voices whispered. "He's going to speak."

When only a minimal buzz of chatter remained, he said into the mic, "Thank you for coming here today. I hope every person among you finds something they can take from what I say. First, let me be clear. I don't have any great truths to reveal, and I'm not here to tell you what you should do with your lives. I don't have all the answers and I've never claimed to. That's because the answer is different for everyone. It lies inside you and it's up to you to find it. All I can do today is maybe give you some clues to help you on your way."

It was his standard patter. He'd said the same thing so many times over so many years he could think about something entirely different while the words fell from his mouth.

He was becoming jaded, beginning to feel bored and frustrated with what he was doing—bored and frustrated with himself. It seemed the more he told people they needed to figure things out for themselves and that *they* controlled their lives and destinies, the more they clung to *him*. If the behavior of his most faithful disciples was anything to go by, his followers were becoming less and less self-determining by the minute no matter what he told them, or was it because of what he told them?

He avoided digital communication of all kinds so he was spared the overflowing inbox and endless messages, but people would come up to him after events like these and ask him for advice on the most inane, ridiculous matters.

A young woman had cornered him just a minute ago backstage.

"I feel like having a pet would make me happier," she'd said. "What do you think, Elek? Would having a pet help me fulfill my inner spirit?"

The pointlessness of what he was attempting and the potential damage he might be causing to people's lives had begun to eat at him.

Yet he couldn't seem to stop. There was something about what he did, the rush of having the attention of thousands of people and the knowledge that he exerted so much power over them was a heady, intoxicating mix. It was hard to resist.

At one point, when he'd begun to question himself and his motivations, Arief had spurred him on and refused to let him quit. That had been a few years ago.

Now, he didn't think he could give up anyway. He was in too deep.

"Consider a newborn baby," he said. "Is it a blank slate? No. Scientists have told us that a new human being is genetically determined in many factors of its life. It has its own little personality just waiting to emerge. It's already its own person. Do we have many parents here tonight?"

About a fifth of the audience's hands shot up.

"You have the most important job in the world. It's your

duty to help your little people grow, to nurture what makes them truly themselves. But the journey doesn't stop there."

And so on, and so on.

Blah, blah, blah.

A disturbance started up near the front of the audience. While one part of his brain worked his mouth, another part watched the churning among the jammed-in people. Someone was forcing a path through the throng, pushing his way toward the stage.

Elek glanced at the wings. They were empty. Arief was not here. Where the hell had he gone? He'd never missed a show before.

Elek's gaze pierced the darkness offstage. Another familiar figure was also absent.

Where was Setia?

Shouts of protest arose as the hooded figure drew nearer the foot of the stage. A security operative moved from the side of the crowd to intercept him.

Elek vaguely remembered Setia giving him a hug last night. She hadn't hugged him in years. What had *that* been about? Had she been saying goodbye?

The major news of the day flashed into his mind. Ua Talman's colonists had begun boarding their ships. Setia had said something about applying to the project months ago. Had she gone ahead and done it? Was she leaving on a colony ship?

The security officer had reached the threatening man in the audience and was in a tussle with him. A collective gasp sounded as the officer slid down, disappearing despite the packed bodies.

The man was at the stage! His hands clasped the edge and he hauled himself up.

Fear paralyzed Elek. He couldn't move, only stare in horror.

The man was carrying a knife, its blade glistening with

fresh blood and an odd metallic glow. Was it Flo Metal? Was that how he'd sneaked the weapon in?

In a great effort of will Elek yelled and raised his arms protectively, backing away.

Everything was happening too fast.

"Setia!"

Where was she? Why wasn't she here to protect him?

The blade flashed down.

EPILOGUE

An old woman was looking out at Taylan from her mirror. Could it really be her? She felt the same inside as she'd always done but her body had aged. She felt duped. She hadn't given permission for this to happen.

Picking up her brush, she sighed.

Oh, well.

It was best to make the most of the time she had left.

She brushed her hair. It was white now, like Arthur's had been the last time she'd seen him. That had been decades ago and very, very far away on a distant planet circling a strange sun. So long ago it all felt like a dream. When she thought back she found it hard to believe she had once worn a suit of armor and fought on a battlefield like the knights of old. It had been as if she'd stepped into a legend, a mythological time that no one was certain had ever really existed.

Things had moved on. When historians studied the events of the war with the Crusaders, they cast doubt on Arthur's existence. The vids, images, and recordings of the king could have been faked, they said, and even if he had been a real person, there was nothing to prove he was *the* King Arthur. He could have been an actor employed by the Alliance or he could have been mentally ill. It was rumored that the BA archives contained medical data and testimony from the time immediately following the discovery of his mummified body, but the archives were sealed for security purposes and no date had been set for opening them.

She knew he'd been real, but she was just an old lady. Whenever she tried to tell anyone her story they listened politely with a fixed expression that said she must be losing her marbles.

What did it all matter now anyway? Her life had been good, all things considered. She'd known a great love and a great king. She'd seen myth come to life. There weren't many who could say the same.

As she gazed vacantly into the mirror's reflection she saw the door behind her opening. Lunch had arrived a little early today.

A different figure from the one she expected walked in, and her brush dropped with a clatter to the dressing table.

It can't be!

Without even registering what she was doing, she found herself on her feet. In three steps her son was in her arms.

"Patrin, is it really you?" She could hardly breathe. Was she dreaming?

"It's really me, Mam."

She held him close, unable to speak.

"I've been back a couple of days," he said. "I couldn't find you at first. It took me a while to get used to the human way of doing things, and I didn't even guess you might be living in a home for seniors." He added, "Er, Mam, you're hurting me."

She released him and took his face in her hands. He looked the same as her last sight of him on a jousting field half a galaxy away and a lifetime ago. Except not quite. His expression was different, his gaze strange. Something inside him had changed.

She said, "I'm glad you found me in the end."

"Me too, Mam. Me too. I missed you so much. I've missed you all. Where's TJ? Is he here as well?"

A too-familiar ache expanded in her heart. "Wright died two years ago."

"No!" Patrin's features fell.

"Don't be sad. I try not to be. It was peaceful and he'd lived a long and happy life. You have nieces and nephews, you know. And grand-nieces and nephews."

"Kayla got married? That's great. What about Carys? What's she been doing? Does she still rescue birds?"

"Carys left on one of Ua Talman's ships. She was long gone by the time we got back. I haven't heard from her since."

Patrin sat down on Taylan's bed, looking forlorn. "I didn't mean to be away so long. Time passes differently there."

Taylan sat next to him. "Where's Arthur? Is he back too?"

"He's gone, Mam. When I decided to come home, he said he wanted to see more of the galaxy, to meet other kinds of life. They'll help him do that."

It was bittersweet news. She would have loved to meet her old friend again, but it felt right that he would be an ambassador for humanity among the stars.

"Arthur said," Patrin went on, "that if Britons ever need him again, he'll return."

"I know he will, sweetheart. Of course he will."

FOLLOW CARYS AND SETIA'S STORY IN THE SPACE
COLONIZATION ADVENTURE
INTERSTELLAR FLEET
BOOK ONE: *TALMAN PRIME*

AUTHOR'S NOTES

Coming to the end of a series is always bittersweet. Usually, the good guys have vanquished their enemies and the rest of their lives promises to be happy and peaceful, but it's also time to say goodbye to characters I've come to know and love.

I couldn't have created Star Legend without the help and support of all my shipmates, especially Liza Wood, Mike Phillips, Mike Paddick, Alex Green, the Review Crew, and Patreon supporters.

Parallels with Arthurian Mythology (and spoilers)

Writing this series was somewhat of a self-indulgence. I've loved Arthurian mythology for as long as I can remember, and it was a joy to revisit the famous characters and old tales. If you're an Arthur nerd too, you probably noticed some parallels. As I hinted in notes on *The Gallant*, the brothers from West BI were inspired by another set of legendary siblings: Sir Gawain, Sir Gaheris, Sir Agravaine, and Sir Gareth. In one of the original stories, Gareth (Marc) remains loyal to Lancelot when the other brothers turn against him due to his affair with Guinevere. When Lancelot storms in to rescue the queen from execution he accidentally kills Gareth—and actually Gaheris too—sparking the surviving brothers' undying hatred.

Another character you might have recognised is Sir Bors, who inspired Abacha. Bors is Lancelot's cousin, constant ally, and aide. He is also one of the few knights to achieve the Sangreal, which leads me to Patrin's story.

The Quest for the Sangreal or Holy Grail is a large part of Arthur's story. In order to restore peace and fecundity to the Isles and cure the wound of the Fisher King, the Knights of the Round Table must seek a sighting of the Sangreal. The problem is, only truly noble and pure knights can achieve it. Lancelot only gains a partial sighting (no puzzle as to why), but his son, Galahad, sees the holy vessel in all its glory. Hence the reason behind Kayla mentioning that her brother had never had a girlfriend. Galahad is also the only knight who can beat Lancelot in a fight.

This is why it was important that Taylan found her children. Only Patrin was capable of defeating Merlin and securing humanity's independence and freedom from interference.

There are more parallels to the great stories scattered throughout the books, some I may have already forgotten. As with all literature, what I as the author intended doesn't really matter. If you saw it, it's there.

Names

Another self-indulgence I confess to is picking names with significant meanings. Elek is the Hungarian short form of Alexis, which is itself a shortened version of Alexander, which means 'defender of man'. Setia is an Indonesian name that means faithful or trustworthy, rather ironically in this case, but she may exemplify her name better in a later series.

Elek's Message

You may have suspected that, when Elek exhorts his followers to be themselves yet also despairs that they only seem to want to be told what to do, I was channelling Life of Brian where Brian tells the crowd they're all individuals. In which case, you would be right.

I hope you've enjoyed reading Taylan and Wright's story as much as I've enjoyed writing it. I may find it hard to let them go just yet and end up writing a short story of an adventure after they return to Earth, or perhaps a tale of what happens to Arthur and Patrin on the alien planet.

But for now it's time to move on. If you'd like to read my latest books a few weeks earlier than they're released to the general public, you can become a patron. I'd really appreciate your support.

To chat about the series or meet other readers, come along to the Starship JJ Green Shipmates Facebook group. I'd love to see you there.

You could also sign up to my reader group for exclusive free books, discounts on new releases, review crew invitations and other interesting stuff:

https://jjgreenauthor.com/free-books/

DOWNLOAD YOUR FREE READERS' GUIDE TO THE SCIENCE FICTION NOVELS OF J.J. GREEN